OUTLAW VENGEANCE

Scout Jeff Malone and his patrol have Jonas Grigg captured and his gang cornered. Concerned over potential casualties from the cross-fire, Malone strikes a deal with the outlaw, allowing him a peaceable departure. But, once free, a humiliated Grigg swears revenge ... Tracing Malone to Rocky Creek, he plans to kill his adversary and rob the town bank. Ominously, mysterious gunmen appear and an acquaintance of Malone is murdered. Can Malone ever hope to destroy the threat of the outlaw's vengeance?

GREG MITCHELL

OUTLAW VENGEANCE

Complete and Unabridged

LINFORD
Leicester

First published in Great Britain in 2006 by
Robert Hale Limited
London

First Linford Edition
published 2006
by arrangement with
Robert Hale Limited
London

The moral right of the author
has been asserted

British Library CIP Data

Mitchell, Greg
    Outlaw vengeance.—Large print ed.—
Linford western library
    1. Outlaws—West (U.S.)—Fiction
    2. Western stories 3. Large type books
    I. Title
    823.9'2 [F]

    ISBN 1–84617–550–X

Published by
F. A. Thorpe (Publishing)
Anstey, Leicestershire

Set by Words & Graphics Ltd.
Anstey, Leicestershire
Printed and bound in Great Britain by
T. J. International Ltd., Padstow, Cornwall

This book is printed on acid-free paper

1

Joe Maxwell squinted down the twin barrels of his shotgun and centred the bead foresight squarely on the chest of the rider who had halted the coach. Though dust from the sudden stop still swirled around, he could see at a glance that this man was no ordinary cowhand.

The rider was young, tall but slightly built. His crumpled grey hat was pulled low over his eyes to shade against the low afternoon sun and the face between hat and red bandanna had been clean-shaven but now sported a week's dark stubble. His clothes were those of a frontiersman, a faded blue shirt and dusty light-brown trousers tucked into long boots, but the stranger had a dangerous look about him. Maxwell could see an ivory-handled revolver on the rider's right hip and its holster hung from a belt filled with cartridges. The brass receiver of his Winchester carbine caught the lowering sun's rays as it swayed in the leather loop attached to the saddle horn. The saddle was not the usual westerner's type. It was a lighter Hope saddle as favoured by some military officers. The man's mount was a fine bay gelding with a white blaze and was guaranteed to attract the attention of any admirer of good horseflesh. Usually only lawmen and military officers who could afford them, or outlaws who could steal them, rode such animals.

Maxwell was overly cautious at the best of times and under these circumstances was in no mood to take chances. The outlaw, Jonas Grigg, was rumoured to be in that part of the country. Beside him, he saw the driver, Bert Olsen transfer his reins to his left hand and move his right hand to his gun butt. He was wary of the strange rider, too.

'Be careful with that cannon,' the rider warned.

'I'll decide how careful I'll be. Who are you? Why have you stopped us?' Maxwell demanded suspiciously.

'I'm Jeff Malone, scouting for the Fifth Cavalry. Major Carter sent me to stop you. A big party of Cheyenne have jumped the reservation. It's not safe to go on.'

'We didn't hear nothin' about that when we left Pronghorn Flats last night,' Olsen said, 'and nobody at the last change station knew about it. We ain't seen the cavalry in these parts either. Last we heard, the Cheyenne were all livin' peaceful on the reservation.'

'You heard wrong,' Malone said bluntly. 'Some of them never went on to the reservation and a lot come and go as they please. I've been up there with the army trying to corral them. This is the biggest breakout yet.'

'How do I know you ain't a road agent? You could be Jonas Grigg for all I

3

know.' The guard was not convinced and had not lowered his shotgun.

'You ain't wearin' buckskins. I figured that all Indian scouts wore buckskins.' The driver also sounded doubtful.

'They only do that in dime novels. Buckskins get too hot.'

'He don't look old enough to be Grigg,' Olsen whispered.

'He could still be one of his gang,' Maxwell said stubbornly.

Malone was tired from hard riding and was growing impatient. He had seen unshod pony tracks earlier in the day and half suspected that a war party could be in the vicinity. A coach in such an area was a tempting target to scalp hunters.

'I don't have all day. You are risking your lives and the lives of your passengers every second you argue. If you have a lick of sense you'll turn this coach around and head back to the last change station. Get yourself killed if you like, but your passengers should

4

have some choice.'

'Passengers don't make company rules,' Olsen announced. 'As driver, I'm in charge here.'

'Not any more,' said a cold voice behind him.

The driver looked down to see one of his passengers, a gambler, who called himself Mark Wilson, leaning out the coach window and holding a small revolver pointed straight at him.

Wilson normally took a casual approach to life, but the driver's arguments in the face of obvious danger had angered him. He decided to settle the issue by direct action.

Olsen sat stunned. He had not expected trouble from someone who appeared as easy-going as Wilson. The big, gruff rancher, McDonald, seemed more likely to dissent, or even the two female members of the three Cranes. Women could be difficult passengers at times, but gamblers were used to taking the rough with the smooth.

Wilson did not waste words. 'There

are five passengers here. We've heard what the scout said and we all agree that we should turn back. I'm quite prepared to blow you off that box if you don't turn this coach around.'

'I'll do it, but you're in trouble. The company's gonna hear of this.'

The gambler gave a grim smile, his eyes cold above the gun's sights. 'If you don't turn this coach around, they sure as hell won't hear it from you.'

Another passenger, the male member of the Crane party called, 'We should turn back, driver. You can't take the risk of going on.'

'Looks like you're overruled, driver,' Malone said. 'I'll ride ahead so you can watch me, if you're that dang suspicious, but your time will be better spent watching for trouble.'

Mumbling under his breath at the lack of respect for his position, but secretly relieved that a difficult decision had been taken out of his hands, Olsen released the brake, shook the reins and swung his team about. If they were robbed or delayed unnecessarily he could always claim that he had been forced at gunpoint to divert the coach.

As Malone cantered his horse around the turning coach, he saw two pretty female faces, one framed by dark hair and the other with fair hair looking anxiously from the coach window. They were a welcome sight after the weather-beaten cavalrymen who had been his constant companions for the past three weeks. Keep your mind on your work, he told himself.

Inside the coach, Nancy Crane brushed her fair curls away from her face and laughingly told her sister-in-law, 'There's a husband for you, Julie.' Nancy was recently married to Tom and thought that Julie had been single too long.

'I suppose I could do worse,' the dark-haired girl said, as though she was really considering the prospect. She knew the reaction she would get from her extremely protective brother.

Tom Crane did not see the joke. As a

railroad surveyor he had seen a few government scouts on the frontier and had seen none that he considered worthy of his younger sister. 'I think you can forget that one, Julie. Some of those scouts are wild men, drunks and gunfighters and only half-civilized. I would not let you marry a man like that.'

Wilson, the gambler, imagined that he had a way with the ladies and joined in the teasing. 'What about me?'

'Certainly not you, Mr Wilson,' Julie laughed. 'I just saw you stick up a coach.'

'I guess that only leaves me,' the other male passenger chuckled. Jason McDonald was a powerfully built, middle-aged man with a neatly trimmed beard and the clothes of an affluent rancher. He had a big Smith & Wesson .44, butt-forward on his left hip and looked as though he knew how to use it. Beneath the affable manner however, McDonald was seething. He had not wanted to turn back and

Wilson's action had surprised him as much as it had surprised the coach driver. Still, he would make the best of a bad situation. There was no point in getting scalped. He joked with his fellow passengers and pretended to be hurt when Julie laughingly turned down his proposal.

Tom Crane was a worried man. His brown eyebrows nearly met as he wrinkled his brow in a frown. Until Malone's arrival he had been enjoying the trip but now he was really worried. During his work on the Union Pacific railroad he had seen the results of Cheyenne raids. He found himself suddenly wanting his Remington hunting rifle that was with the baggage in the boot. The thought of his wife and sister falling into Cheyenne hands completely eclipsed his concerns about his own fate.

Faced with a longer stage and with his team already tired, Olsen held the six horses to a steady trot. Malone, riding about fifty yards ahead, kept the bay horse to the same pace. It was not a relaxing ride for anyone. The coach road ran through a landscape of rolling, sage-covered hills with occasional thickets of scrub oak and cedar. Here and there rocky outcrops projected from the red soil adding to the number of places where ambushers could lurk. The plume of dust thrown up by the horses and coach wheels would attract the attention of observers miles away and those in the right places could easily set a trap for the travellers.

The sun was sinking, throwing long shadows across the ground when Malone glanced to his left and saw a glint of metal on a distant hill. He watched but the reflection did not come again. Whatever had caught the sun's rays had moved.

He checked his horse and pulled off the road till the coach came abreast. He pointed to the hill.

'There's someone up there. I just saw the sun glinting on metal. It could be some stray Cheyenne. How far are we from the change station?'

'About two miles,' Maxwell shouted back.

'That hill's about a mile away so we have a bit of a start. It might be an idea if we pick up the pace a bit. The sooner we get a few walls around us, the safer I'll feel,' Malone called.

'I'm the driver here,' Olsen growled. 'I say what the pace is to be.' He held the team to the same pace until he felt that he had made his point and then urged them to greater speed.

The scout was worried. The light was failing quickly and soon it would be too dark to see any pursuers or warriors lurking ahead of them in ambush. While Indians did not like fighting in the dark, he knew that they would risk it if the chances of being killed were minimal. The prospect of scalps and loot often outweighed the fear of being killed at night and wandering forever in darkness.

The team was tiring visibly when the coach topped the hill from which the Two Wells station could be seen. The buildings and corrals showed as an indistinct blur half a mile away in the gloom.

'Somethin's wrong,' Olsen told Maxwell. 'No lights are showin'.'

The guard called to Malone, 'Hold up a bit. Might be trouble ahead.'

When the scout rode over to the coach, Olsen leaned down and told him, 'The change station is only about half a mile ahead. They should have the lamps lit by now. Somethin's wrong.'

Malone spoke softly, 'Wait here. I'll have a look around. Keep as quiet as possible. Sound carries a long way out here. If you hear shooting turn around and try to find a place to fort up. If all is right, I'll strike a match or show a light of some kind. Be a bit patient because I'll be creeping in there and it could take me a while.'

'What if they get you before you can shoot?' the driver asked.

'I'll have a cocked gun in my hand and the odds are against them getting me so quick and quiet that I can't pull a trigger. But if they do, you'll need to figure out something else.'

Tom Crane looked out of the coach window. 'It seems to me that you are taking on a very dangerous job here, Mr Malone. Is there any way round this situation?'

'Not really,' the scout replied. 'A coach and six horses are hard to hide but easy to stop, one leader down and the whole shebang crashes. It's best if you keep out of danger until we know the lie of the land.'

'But it's not fair that one person should take all the risks,' Crane argued. 'What if I go with you?'

'Thanks for the offer but if things go wrong at the station, every man will be needed here. The army pays me two dollars a day for doing this sort of thing and I've had a bit of practice at it.'

Quietly the scout moved his mount off the trail and walked it through the brush where there was less chance of being seen. He rode watchfully with a drawn six-shooter in his hand, his eyes swivelling from one pool of shadow to another. Periodically he would pause and listen, his senses straining to detect the first sign of danger.

After ten nervous minutes he was at the edge of the brush so he dismounted and hitched his horse behind a couple of low trees. He could see a barn nearby, its side windows two squares of blackness. If anyone was in the building, he would have little chance of seeing them. He could only hope that he had not been observed. Moving silently, using the shelter of scattered, low bushes, Malone crept to where he could see that the building's double doors were gaping open.

A large horse corral was between the barn and the adobe-walled station building. The corral was empty and, as he moved into the shadow of the barn wall, the scout could see that its gate was wide open. Taking a chance he slipped through the barn door. To his intense relief, he found himself alone.

From a window he studied the station building. It was dark and silent and the front door was closed. If anyone was watching from inside, they would have an easy shot at him as he left the barn and ran swiftly to the station door. Half expecting a shot in his direction, he sprinted for the building. Pressed against a side wall, he listened but heard no sound from inside. The latch string on the door was out so he cocked his gun and with his left hand lifted the latch and threw open the door.

Relief flooded through him as no gun blazed and no war cry broke the silence. Moving more confidently, Malone checked the few rooms in the building and when he was sure that he was alone, he struck a match and lit the lamp beside the station door. Then he went to retrieve his horse. He had unsaddled the animal and was feeding it some stage company oats when the coach rumbled up to the corral.

'Where's Somers an' the other two?' Olsen demanded, as he halted his team.

He glared pointedly at the bay horse eating company fodder.

'I don't know. The place seems deserted,' Malone replied. He ignored the driver's disapproval. The horse had earned the feed it was eating and while he was on army business he was allowed to commander fodder for his mount.

'Do you reckon it could be Indians?' Maxwell asked. He still held the scattergun ready for trouble. Change stations were usually places of frantic activity and it worried him to see it so silent.

Malone shook his head. 'The place doesn't look wrecked. I think something scared them and they took off.'

2

'Step down, folks,' Olsen called. 'Go inside and make yourselves at home. If that no-good Somers left any grub we might be able to get ourselves a meal.'

Talking among themselves, the passengers alighted, stretched to get the stiffness from their limbs and made their way uncertainly to the gloomy, low-roofed building.

While the passengers went inside the stage station, Malone helped Olsen with the horses.

'Somers's buckboard is gone,' the driver told him, as they unharnessed the team. 'Looks like all three of 'em took off on it. Why do you reckon they did that?'

Malone led a coach horse to the water trough and watched it start drinking before replying. 'I'm guessing that a Cheyenne war party must have run off the spare horses in the corral and your people decided to get while the going was good. Probably reckoned their chances were better if they joined forces with the men at the next station. Let's hope the Cheyenne didn't catch them on the trail somewhere.'

It took a while to unharness the team, hang the harness where it would not become tangled and water the horses. After that they placed each one in a stall with a manger of feed.

Maxwell joined them just as they were about to close the barn doors. He had come to collect the strong box from the coach. 'There's a lot of money in this. Can't afford to leave it lyin' about.' He grunted a little as he lifted the small but heavy box and added, 'Them Crane gals are fixing us a meal from the supplies that Somers left. They said to come for a feed as soon as you are finished here.'

It was then that Malone remembered that he had not eaten since early morning and breakfasts in cavalry camps were hardly lavish. He was ravenous by the time the last horses had been fed and stabled. His mind was still on food as he walked with the driver and guard from the barn.

A sound carried through the evening stillness. It could have just been a stray breeze in the nearby brush, but in Malone's line of work it did not pay to take chances. The coachmen had not noticed it, but Malone stopped and listened. More sounds followed, regular sounds in quick succession. It was the sound of horses moving through the nearby brush. They were not in a hurry but there was no doubt about where they were headed.

He froze and listened, hoping at first that it was his imagination. But there was no mistaking it and the sounds were coming steadily closer.

'There are riders in the brush,' he whispered to Olsen. 'Run for the station door. My carbine's in the barn. I'll head for there.'

The driver snorted in alarm like a

nervous horse then set out for the station building with a speed that denied his fifty plus years. Juggling the strongbox, Maxwell followed closely on his heels.

Malone ran back through the barn doors and risked vital seconds securing them behind him. The faint light from a window showed where his saddle was resting on the edge of a stall and he felt relief course through him as his hand closed around the Winchester's butt. Levering a cartridge into the breech, he hurried to the window closest to the brush.

Crackling twigs and the snuffle of a horse sounded distinctly in the night stillness. There was more than one rider and, given the circumstances, they were likely to be Cheyenne warriors. But he could not shoot until he was sure that the riders were hostile.

'Who's there?' the scout challenged.

An indistinct murmur of voices as if the strangers had been caught by surprise, then a man called back, 'Don't shoot, we're friendly. We're volunteers from Blue Creek. We're looking for the coach and figured you folks could do with some help.'

'We sure could. Come on in.'

Four riders, one leading a saddled horse, appeared out of the gloom and Malone left the barn to open the corral gate for them.

As they filed through the gate, Malone asked, 'Have you seen any Indians?'

'We saw a big war party from a distance a couple of hours ago,' the foremost rider told him. He was tall and thin with two six-shooters and crossed cartridge belts. The others too, were heavily armed and all were well mounted.

Malone indicated the riderless horse. 'Looks like they got one of you.'

Another rider said, 'Hell, no. We made sure they didn't see us. We found this horse wandering loose. Figured he might have got away from here. We weren't sure where the coach would be but then we saw it heading back for the change station.'

'That must have been you we saw on the ridge. We were worried that it was a party of Cheyenne. I don't know where that loose horse came from though. If it was from the station, something happened before we got here. I'm a scout sent by the army to turn the coach back. Unsaddle your horses and come over to the station building when you're ready. There are some folks over there who will be mighty glad to see you.'

'It's nice to know the army are close by,' the tall, skinny rider said, as he dismounted.

'Sure is,' agreed his companion, a man of medium size whose clothing was neater and better quality than the others.

'The cavalry are not all that close. I left them about thirty miles away to the north of here. They sent me to warn the coach to turn back.'

'Lucky they did,' another newcomer

said, as he stepped down stiffly from his mount.

'While you're seeing to your horses,' Malone said, 'I'll warn the cooks that we'll need more food.'

* * *

'Who are those men at the corral?' Tom Crane asked, when Malone rejoined them.

'Said they were from Blue Creek, a volunteer posse of some kind looking for us. Must have heard of the Cheyenne trouble. They came at just the right time.'

Maxwell looked puzzled. 'Blue Creek's a long way away. They must have heard about the Indians days ago to get all the way down here.'

Malone thought for a while. 'I don't see how they could have. The army only picked up their tracks yesterday. Something's not quite right there. Maybe I heard wrong.'

His thoughts were interrupted as Julie Crane emerged from the kitchen with an apron improvised from some sort of kitchen cloth and pressed a tin cup of coffee into the scout's hand. 'I think you need this, Mr Malone,' she said with a smile.

'Thank you. I'm Jeff.'

The smile returned. 'I'm Julie. You have done a lot for us today, thank you.' As Malone sipped the coffee, she pressed a biscuit into his other hand. 'These were left by the station staff. They might be a bit stale but it will be a while before Nancy and I can get a meal together.'

'I hope the crew left enough for four more visitors. The new men at the barn might need feeding.'

'There's something odd about them. They aren't unsaddling, and don't seem in a hurry to come up,' Wilson observed from his place at a window. 'They're going into the barn.'

'I hope they ain't stealin' company feed for their horses,' Olsen growled and looked sharply at Malone as he did so.

'They could be robbing the bags we left on the coach,' Tom Crane suggested.

'Probably just looking for places to put their horses away,' McDonald said casually.

'It's mighty strange behaviour though,' Olsen growled suspiciously. 'I think I should go down there and protect company property.'

'You could get a window in your skull doing that,' Maxwell warned.

Wilson was the first one to realize the true situation. The strangers had lit a lantern from the barn to aid them as they moved about inside. As one man held the light high, his features were clearly visible. The light shone on a craggy face with a neat goatee beard.

A startled gasp came from the gambler. 'That's Clem Ryan. I've seen him before. I saw him shoot a man in Dodge City. Something's wrong. That sure as hell ain't a volunteer posse.'

'Who's Clem Ryan?' Tom Crane asked.

'He's Jonas Grigg's right-hand man. That's the Grigg gang! I'll bet they're searching for the strongbox. That's why they're taking so long in the barn.'

'Good job I brought it with me,' Maxwell muttered, as though quite pleased with his forethought.

'Like hell it was. They'll come here now,' Crane told him.

Malone caught movement out of the corner of his eye. He turned as McDonald suddenly went for his gun.

'Nobody m — '

The gun was clear of its holster but he never finished his command as the scout's fist smashed into his jaw and sent him reeling. As the man fell, Malone drew his gun and covered him. 'Bar that door,' he snapped. Cocking the weapon he pointed it at the man on the floor. 'If you as much as twitch, you're dead.'

'They're coming,' Wilson said urgently.

Maxwell moved like lightning, slamming the door shut and dropping a solid wooden bar into its brackets.

'You're crazy. I was just trying to help,' McDonald protested, as he raised himself on one elbow. He smiled disarmingly. 'I'm no hold-up man.'

'I think you are,' Malone told him. 'That spare horse is for you. I should have shot you . . . probably might have to yet. Don't push your luck.'

The affable rancher suddenly was gone. With hate blazing from his eyes, the man on the floor snarled. 'No man hits Jonas Grigg and lives, Malone. You're as good as dead.'

'So that's who you are. You're very close to getting a bullet through you, Grigg. If you make one suspicious move I'll be happy to put a hole in you.'

The scout picked up the outlaw's fallen revolver and passed it to Wilson who was hovering nearby. 'You might need this.' Then, with a cocked gun at the outlaw's head, he searched his prisoner but to his surprise found no other weapon.

'They're just outside,' Nancy Crane called from the window.

Maxwell snatched up his shotgun and pulled back its large rabbit-ear hammers. 'They ain't gettin' the strong box.'

'Don't start any shooting,' Crane told him urgently, as he pushed his wife away from the window.

'It's a trap, Clem!'

Grigg's warning shout reached the gang and with reflexes honed by constant danger, they split apart and sprinted for cover.

The shotgun boomed twice but only raised a harmless cloud of dust from the trampled ground. The restriction of the narrow window had prevented free movement on the shooter's part and both barrels missed.

From outside, guns began firing. A bullet tore a long splinter from the window frame sending the guard ducking away from the opening.

Olsen kept well away from the window but joined in the shooting by blindly firing a couple of wild shots from his Navy Colt. They did no execution but served notice that the station would be stoutly defended.

In the confined space, the noise of the guns was bad enough, but the acrid fumes of the powder smoke stung eyes and quickly started coughing among some of the defenders.

'Throw your guns down while you're still alive,' Grigg shouted at them. 'We only want the strong box. Those boys out there are too good for you.'

Malone cocked his Colt. 'Shut up.' Then he called to Wilson, 'Keep an eye on Grigg. Shoot him if he makes a doubtful move. I'll check the back of the building.'

'It will be a pleasure,' Wilson said. 'The reward on Grigg says dead or alive and he'll be a lot less trouble if he's dead.'

'You're dead too, tinhorn,' the outlaw threatened.

Wilson did not bluff easily and now with Grigg's own gun in his hand he was sure that he held all the aces. 'I'll live long enough to let daylight through you, Grigg, and with your own gun too.'

Malone snatched up his carbine. 'Watch the windows,' he called, and ran to the kitchen. He knew that such buildings always had back doors and was sure that the outlaws would have similar thoughts. The two women were crouched on the floor. Bullets were thudding into walls and adobe chips and dust were being gouged from them. Powder smoke drifting in from the main area hung in the air.

The building had a back door opening from the kitchen and, as the scout had guessed, it was not barred. He flipped over the long table sending food and dishes crashing but the heavy planks gave some protection to the women. 'Stay down,' he called, above the roar of gunfire from the other room.

A split second later the back door was kicked in and a tall, thin man with a gun in each hand appeared in the doorway. Both women screamed in terror.

Malone fired the carbine from the hip and the outlaw collapsed on the step. One of his guns exploded sending a bullet into the roof as it slipped from nerveless fingers. The scout levered another shell into the rifle's breech and put a second shot into his victim who was stirring feebly. He could not risk being shot later by the wounded man.

Crane appeared at the inner doorway clutching the small revolver he had been given by Wilson. 'Are you both all right?' he asked, breathlessly, as he crouched beside his wife and sister.

'One tried to break in,' Nancy said nervously. 'I think Mr Malone killed him.'

'Are you OK, Jeff?' Crane whispered.

'I'm OK. Keep your gun on that door and shoot anyone you see there. I'll try to get you a better gun,' the scout said softly.

Keeping well away from the open doorway, he crept across to the fallen man. A large open-top Colt, similar to his own lay near the body. He tucked the weapon in his belt and unbuckled one of the dead man's cartridge belts. The buckle for the second belt was out of his reach and he had no intention of getting himself shot while trying to reach it. The revolver he picked up had been modified to take metallic cartridges and would be an asset to the defenders' armoury. Frontier gunsmiths had modified many earlier-model revolvers to take the .44 rimfire round used in the Winchester and Henry rifles. Metallic cartridges could be centre-fire or rim-fire making it necessary to select the ammunition for which the weapon had been altered. Malone's own Colt was a centre-fire but a quick feel of the captured cartridges showed them to be rim-fires. It was a bit of a struggle to get the belt out from under the dead man but he finally managed it. With his prize he crawled back to the Cranes.

'Here's a better gun and some ammunition for it. Have you used a

Colt with these metallic cartridges?'

'I haven't, but I know how they load them.'

'Good. Keep that door covered.'

'Give me the little gun,' Julie said, as she tried bravely to keep a quiver out of her voice. 'I can shoot a gun.'

'Good for you, Julie, but don't shoot until you are sure that you can hit your man,' Malone whispered. 'I'll have to see what's happening at the front but I'll be back soon.'

The defenders had organized themselves in the front rooms. The stage crew had each covered a window and Wilson had moved his prisoner to a windowless sleeping area off the main dining-place.

Maxwell had a bloody groove on his left forearm and had fired off the last of his shotgun shells. He now clutched a big Remington revolver.

'How are things here?' Malone asked.

'We're keepin' 'em away but are getting a mite short of pistol cartridges. We never carry many on the coach.

Olsen's down to his last couple of shots, too.'

'You inside,' a voice called from the darkness. 'We want to talk.'

'No one's stopping you,' Malone called back. 'What do you want?'

'Is Grigg still alive?'

'He is, but in case you're wondering, your long, skinny friend isn't, and at the first sign of trouble, Grigg won't be either. What do you want?'

'We want Grigg and the strong box and we'll ride out of here.'

'Not a chance.'

'Don't be a fool. You'll run out of ammunition before we do. We can wait.'

'We have your boss. We'll kill him if this attack keeps up. Maybe he's prepared to offer a deal.'

'You strike a deal with Jonas and we'll stick to it.'

The outlaw chief heard the exchange and called from the back room, 'Do as he says, Malone. There are still three top-class gun hands out there. A lot of people will die over this. Let's try to sort this out with a minimum of shooting.'

Much as he hated to admit it, the scout recognized the truth of Grigg's words. The defenders had the numbers but the attackers were well-armed professionals, with a supply of ammunition that almost certainly would outlast their own.

'We're waiting for an answer,' the voice called again, impatiently this time.

'What do you think?' the scout asked the coach crew.

'They ain't getting the box,' Maxwell declared.

'We have to think of lives here,' Olsen told him.

Maxwell set his jaw and adopted a defiant stance. 'There ain't no way I'm gonna give up this box. No two-bit outlaws are takin' it while I'm alive.'

'We can't avoid casualties forever,' Malone argued. 'There might not be many left on either side if this thing is fought through to the end. We aren't in a position to withstand a long fight. If we can make a deal, it might be the only way out of this mess. I think that Grigg is our best bargaining chip. Let's see what he has to offer.' He raised his voice and called to the captured outlaw, 'What's your best offer, Grigg? Remember, if things have to be fought out you're going to be the first one shot.'

'Whatever terms I make, Malone, they don't apply to you. Nobody hits me and lives.'

'Give us your best offer and remember, your life hangs on it.'

'This is my one offer and I don't give a damn if you take it or leave it. Keep the strongbox, let me go and I'll take my men out of here.'

Malone thought for a while. 'How can we trust you?'

'You can trust me on this. It took me a long time to get this crew together and I don't want to lose any more of them. There'll be other strongboxes.'

'What do you reckon?' Malone asked the coach driver.

'It's better than innocent folks getting killed.'

'Right, Grigg, call out your proposal to your men.'

'Can you hear me, Clem?'

'I can hear you, Jonas.'

'The deal is that they release me and we ride away. I reckon we've lost this hand. Will you and the boys agree to it?'

'If you say so, Jonas. How are they going to play it?'

'We'll work that out and get back to you,' Malone shouted.

A few minutes later the defenders had worked out a plan.

The scout ordered Grigg, 'Tell them that at daylight they leave a saddled horse for you in the corral. They are to ride up the road to that hilltop where we can see them. It's out of carbine range so they will be safe. When we see them there, you can walk to your horse and ride away.'

Grigg shouted out the conditions and the other outlaw agreed to them. Then, nervous and on the verge of exhaustion, the defenders settled down to wait.

3

Malone relieved Wilson who had been guarding the prisoner. The gambler was a brave man but his over-confident casual attitude was a worry. A man like Grigg needed to be watched carefully. They had bound his hands, but more than one man had managed to slip out of ropes.

'I didn't expect to find a famous outlaw travelling by coach,' the scout said, as he sat on a wooden stool with his gun drawn, just out of reach of the prisoner.

'Neither did anyone else. Clem and the boys were to meet the coach at the next station and I would already have had the guard covered. You ruined a good plan and threw a spoke in my wheel with your Indian scare that turned us back too soon, but Clem's smart and I knew that he'd come looking for us.'

'You're only half our problem, Grigg. The Cheyenne are still out there somewhere. They might jump us, or you and your men on the trail in the morning.'

'That prospect doesn't scare me, Malone. Any Indians who heard tonight's gun battle would reckon that the cavalry were having it out with a few of their friends and would get to hell out of the place.'

'Don't be too sure. If it was a big war party, they might have decided to take a hand. They like to attack at dawn. For all we know, they could be creeping up on these buildings right now.'

'They'll get a shock if they take on Clem and the boys.'

'We have managed to hold them off so far,' Malone reminded him. 'If the Indians should drive your men off, there will be no deal. We won't let you go if we don't have to.'

'You could join us, Malone. It's an easier life than scouting for the army and the money's good. I've heard that there's more than ten thousand dollars in the strongbox here. Join us and I can guarantee you two thousand straight away.'

'Save your breath, Grigg. I'm not interested.'

'You're a fool, Malone. If you join us I'll call it quits between us but if you keep going the way you are, I'll hunt you down and kill you as slowly as I can. You have never had an enemy like me. Think well before you do something that you are certain to regret.'

'Keep your trap shut, Grigg. You are giving me a very good reason to shoot you here and now. Don't talk yourself into a bullet.'

Aware that the scout's patience was wearing thin, Grigg wisely fell silent.

Though the defenders tried to organize short periods of sleep, nobody managed more than a few minutes. With the kitchen door held open by the dead bandit it was too dangerous for Nancy and Julie to try preparing food. Through the night they had drunk the last of the water inside the station and none dared risk a trip to the well near the horse corral. When the darkness finally began to fade into day, all were hungry, thirsty and close to exhaustion.

'Are you there, Jonas?' Ryan called from the barn.

'I'm here, Clem.'

'Let's get this deal settled. The horses are all saddled and ready.'

Malone left Tom Crane guarding the outlaw and moved to a window. 'Bring out Grigg's horse and hitch it to the corral gate. Then ride to the top of that hill to the north where the trail crosses it. When I see the three of you up there, I'll release him. If any property has been taken from the baggage on the coach, it has to be put back or the deal's off.'

Seconds later, a short, broad-shouldered man with a red beard, led a saddled horse out of the stable. Cautiously he walked to the corral gate and hitched the animal there. Then, as if expecting to be attacked at any minute, he backed away, his hands hovering close to the pair of guns that he wore. Seeing no hostile actions from the defenders, his companions emerged and stood widely spaced, alert for any trouble. When one man had mounted and ridden out of range, the next mounted his horse while his comrade stood ready for any surprise attack. They had no intention of all being cut down at once in a sudden hail of lead.

Ryan was the last one to ride away. A man of medium size, he had the hard face and cold eyes of a killer. A large drooping moustache covered his upper lip and he sported a small, goatee beard. He saw himself as a bit of a dandy and tried to foster a romantic image that did not go with his dark deeds. When he saw the women watching from the window, he removed his black stetson with its white horse-hair band and made an exaggerated bow from the saddle.

'It looks like you have won another

heart,' Nancy joked to Julie.

'That skunk don't have a heart,' Wilson muttered. 'He kills people for fun.'

A couple of anxious minutes dragged by and Maxwell called. 'They're all on the hilltop. I can see 'em.'

Malone gestured with his gun. 'Time to go, Grigg.'

Relieved at the prospect of freedom but humiliated by the failure of his plan, the outlaw made one attempt to embarrass Malone. 'You know we could settle this man-to-man outside, Malone. Just give me a gun and we'll prove who's the better man in a fair fight.'

The scout was not fooled. 'We know who the better man is, Grigg, and I'm in no hurry to find out who the better shot is. You and I are going out there now and you can get on a horse and ride away, and think yourself lucky that you came out of this only losing one man.'

'And your gun,' Wilson reminded

43

him, as he pulled his coat aside to reveal that he was wearing Grigg's big Smith & Wesson.

A look of fury crossed the outlaw's face but he controlled it quickly. 'Malone is already as good as dead, and you, my tinhorn friend are the same. I will hunt you both down.'

'I'm really scared,' Wilson said in mock alarm.

'There's a horse waiting for you, but first we'll see what damage your thieving friends have done in the barn.' Malone growled.

'I'll come with you,' Tom Crane said.

They marched the prisoner between them to the barn and checked inside. The bandits had rifled the baggage and scattered clothing about but the coach and the horses had been not been harmed.

Crane was relieved to find that his prized rifle had not been taken. 'I thought your men would have taken this rifle,' he told Grigg.

The outlaw chuckled. 'You'd never

make a bank robber, sonny. A single-shot, long-range rifle isn't much use to us. Our repeaters might not have the range but they can throw a lot of lead in a hurry. My boys travel light and we don't load our horses with anything we can't use.' He turned to Malone and, in a voice laden with sarcasm, asked, 'Do you mind greatly if I go now?'

'No doubt your small-time thieving friends have taken a few items from the bags but it is worth that to be rid of you. The sooner you're gone, Grigg, the happier I'll be and the better this place will smell. I'll take you to your horse.'

They walked to the fine black gelding that his henchmen had left for the outlaw.

'Nice horse,' Malone observed. 'I wonder where you stole him from.'

Grigg glowered and took the reins. Anger showed on his face as he stepped into the saddle. He turned and glared at Malone. 'I'll see you again.' Then he wheeled the horse and galloped away.

'What makes me think that I haven't

made a friend there?' the scout chuckled, as they walked back to the station.

Grigg reined in when he reached his men on the hill-top and glared back at the distant buildings. He was toying with the idea of having another try at the defenders and this time revenge was the overwhelming motive.

'What went wrong, Jonas?' Ryan asked. 'I thought with you on the inside we'd have the game by the throat. Even when the Indians forced a slight change of plans, that job looked easy.'

'A tinhorn named Wilson recognized you when you lit the lantern in the stable and that Indian scout, Malone, got the drop on me. I'm going to get that pair. Have you got my other .44?'

'It's in your saddle-bag. Are you thinking of going back?'

'Just for a while I was, but we could lose men. We've already lost Dakota.'

'What happened?' asked Bill Wilkes, the red-bearded man. He and Dakota had joined the gang together two years before.

'That scout, Malone, got him. He must have figured someone would try the back door while all the shooting was at the front. He was there when Dakota busted his way in.' Grigg looked around at Ryan. 'Now, what's the situation?'

'It ain't good, Jonas. We've got no grub because we figured to get some from the stage station after the robbery and we needed to travel light. As well as that we're mighty short of cash. We need to do a job pretty soon.'

'Amen to that,' said Earl Winchell, the fourth outlaw leading the spare horse.

As the outlaws turned their horses to ride away, Wilkes looked at his friend's empty saddle. 'If you don't get that Malone, Jonas, I sure will.'

'I'll get him,' the leader promised grimly.

★   ★   ★

47

Wilson was waiting at the station holding the outlaw's revolver and gunbelt when the scout rejoined them. 'You captured him, Malone. I figure these belong to you.'

'I don't want them. I prefer my Colt any day. The hammer on a Smith & Wesson is harder to reach than that on a Colt and their balance is different. You might still need a good gun so keep it if you like. The Cheyenne could still be around.'

'Thanks, Malone. It could be worth a lot of money. It's not every day you see a gun taken off a famous outlaw.'

'I wouldn't hold on to that gun too long, Wilson. Grigg means what he says and that gun could lead him straight to you.'

The gambler laughed. 'You worry too much. The West is a big place.'

'It sure is,' Malone agreed, 'but if stories are right, Grigg has been all over it. I'm not sure I did you any favours giving you that gun.'

'Like I just said, Malone, you worry

48

too much. Grigg's been hunted since the end of the Civil War. That's eight years. My business is in playing the odds, and the odds are that he has used up his luck by now. Some lawman will catch up with him some day soon.'

'For both our sakes, I hope you're right.'

'What do you reckon we do now?' Tom Crane asked. Although nobody had elected him, the others had come to regard Malone as their leader. Even Olsen seemed to accept that for all his skill in driving, he was out of his depth in the situation in which they had found themselves.

'We stay wide awake,' the scout told them. 'There's no guarantee that Grigg has given up and the Cheyenne could still be about. Keep a sharp lookout and keep your guns handy.'

Julie made one suggestion. 'If somebody will remove that dead man from the kitchen doorway, Nancy and I will try to get some food organized.'

Malone and Maxwell removed the

corpse from the doorway while Olsen took a shovel from the barn and started digging a shallow grave. They retrieved the outlaw's second gun that had fallen outside the building along with his other cartridge belt. The guard appropriated these as he had only two cartridges left in his old cap-and-ball Remington.

'I was always wantin' one of these new-fangled guns but they're a bit hard to come by. Are these cartridges the same as the .44 rim-fire rifle rounds?'

'They are. You'll find that you won't get the misfires that the old paper cartridges were prone to. You can still get the odd misfire with rim-fire cartridges, but they are not common. Now, help me turn this character over and we'll try to see who he was.'

A search of the dead man revealed the usual contents of a frontiersman's pockets, a small amount of money, cigarette makings, matches and a pocket knife. A worn billfold contained a well-creased reward notice for Rube

Grace, also known as Dakota Collins.

'The description on the notice fits this *hombre*,' Maxwell said. 'Says here he's worth five hundred dollars. You might have struck it rich, Malone.'

'I killed him because he needed killing. I'm no bounty hunter.'

They buried the dead outlaw with few regrets and little ceremony before going to drink and wash at the well. Their thirsts slaked and the residue of powder fumes washed from their throats, the men headed for the kitchen where the smell of frying bacon reminded them of how hungry they were.

Julie and Nancy had restored enough of the damaged kitchen to prepare a meal of bacon, biscuits and coffee.

'I sure enjoyed that,' Wilson said, when he had finished his breakfast.

'I hope you did,' Julie said, 'because we are now out of food.'

'Where do we go from here?' Crane asked.

'The horses are fed and rested. I say

we should go on,' Olsen said.

'Grigg and his friends went that way,' Malone reminded him. 'Next time you might not be so lucky.'

'We could always go back,' the gambler suggested. Then he smiled ruefully. 'I just remembered though that there are a few bad losers back in Pronghorn Flats and maybe my chances would be better with Grigg.'

'Don't bet on it,' Maxwell growled. His bullet-grazed arm was sore, and he was not in the best of moods. Nancy had washed the wound in warm salt water and bandaged it but could do little to ease the pain.

Julie had her say then. 'As I recall, Grigg was not the real problem. The danger was that we were likely to be attacked by Indians. Until we know that the Indian problem has been solved, we could run into trouble no matter which way we go. I think we should wait here a bit longer.'

'I agree,' Malone told them. 'We might get hungry but we won't die of starvation if we stay here for another day or so. I might be able to hunt us up some game.'

'That sounds like good sense to me,' Crane said.

'Another day's rest won't hurt the horses,' Olsen said in resignation. He reckoned that the chaos in the stage-line office would not get any worse than it probably was.

4

Nancy had been taking her turn on watch spying out the landscape from the loft of the barn. The party had shared out the various tasks between them and the women had insisted on taking a turn as look-out. The monotony of the job and the lack of sleep gradually wore her down and she found herself nodding. She might have slept for minutes or seconds, she was never really sure, but she awoke with a start. As her head cleared, she saw a dust cloud rising from the flat country to the west. She was sure that horses were making the dust although the distance was too great to see any details.

'Horses!' she shouted in alarm. 'Horses coming from over there.'

Malone had been dozing on some hay in a horse stall and came awake instantly. He snatched up his carbine and bounded up the ladder to the loft. 'Where are they?'

Alarm had temporarily robbed Nancy of her voice. Her face pale, she pointed out of the opening.

'That's horses for sure.' The scout recognized the high, light dust cloud characteristic of mounted men. 'Run back to the house and make sure that everyone is ready. Tell Wilson or Maxwell that I need another gun over here. We have to keep them out of the barn so they can't use it as a place for launching an attack on the station. Run, Nancy, there's not much time.'

The barn would be hard to defend with just two guns but the scout was gambling that a show of force might persuade any raiders that they were best left alone.

Wilson sprinted across the corral, entered the barn and barred the door behind him. 'Where do you want me, Malone?' He sounded eager for the fight to commence.

'Stay down there and stop anyone trying to get through the windows. I can use my carbine best from up here.'

'How many are there?'

'I can't see for sure but from the size of the dust cloud, there's enough to give us trouble.'

He watched anxiously and gradually he could discern a few details about the approaching riders. Relief flooded through him. 'It's a cavalry patrol,' he shouted. 'Warn the others not to shoot. We're safe now.'

The gambler opened the barn doors and called to those in the station. 'It's a cavalry patrol. Nobody shoot.'

Minutes later, the horsemen were there. Malone knew their leader, a little Irish sergeant named Dinny Casey. Eight troopers, their uniforms dusty and stained, rode behind in pairs. All were unshaven and looked weary. Their ribby horses had seen hard usage and were covered in dust and sweat. A couple at the rear with their heads low seemed scarcely able to drag themselves along.

The scout walked out to greet them.

'So here you are, Malone,' the sergeant said. 'The major said I'd find you somewhere along the stage route. You missed all the excitement.'

'What happened?'

'We got on to a big party of Cheyenne and had a running fight with them. We killed a couple but eventually they gave us the slip.'

'Did you lose any men?'

'Not a man, though there were a few new recruits that I would have happily lost. Sure I don't know how we will ever make soldiers out of some of them, so I don't.'

'You didn't have all the fun, Dinny. We've had our own excitement here with road agents. Did you see any civilian riders on the way here?'

'Not a one. What happened?'

'Get down and I'll tell you, but first come and meet the people you have just rescued. Though before you do, do you have any orders for me?'

'That I do. Major Carter wants you to join him on the north fork of Sandy Creek. He'll be along there somewhere. You'll find his tracks.'

'What are you doing here, Dinny?'

'These are the weakest horses in the command. There's precious little campaigning left in them. I was sent to find the stagecoach and escort it back to Pronghorn Flats. If one of these horses looks like giving out, I can put the rider on the coach. They've had a lot of hard work in the last couple of days and some of these new men are not very good riders. There's one there that would give a rocking horse a sore back, so he would. That black horse that Heinze is riding is as old as me. He should have been pensioned years ago.'

'The government certainly isn't spending up big on the military.'

'That's for sure, Malone. The folks back East think that all the Indians are now happily sitting on reservations and see no need to spend money on soldiers. If only they knew. Some of these men are hopeless shots because we don't have enough spare ammunition to give them target practice.'

While the troopers were attending to their horses, the scout took Casey over to where the coach travellers were waiting. He introduced him and then announced, 'Sergeant Casey will look after you now and escort you back to Pronghorn Flats. I have to go north to join the command again.'

'We'll be sorry to see you go,' Crane told him. 'I think everyone agrees that you did a good job here. We owe you a lot.'

Malone looked embarrassed and shrugged his shoulders. 'I don't think I'll be popular in some quarters for letting Jonas Grigg escape.'

'You helped save the coach's strongbox and kept us all alive,' Julie said. 'Surely innocent lives are worth more than that outlaw.'

'That might be the case, but how many more innocent lives will Grigg take after I let him go?' Malone reminded her.

'You worry too much, Malone,' Wilson said. 'You have to play the cards that are dealt you and you did the best anyone could do with the hand you had.'

Julie put a hand on his arm. 'I hope we meet again some day. Tom's opening a surveying business at Rocky Creek. If you are ever up that way, call in and see us.'

The scout said, 'I might do that, ma'am.' But he doubted that their paths would cross again. He was sorry because he felt that he could easily spend the rest of his life with this girl. He liked everything about her. Already though, realism was telling him that he had little to offer her and his future could be a short one.

'I hope we meet again, Jeff,' Julie said softly, as though she too was reluctant to see him go.

'So do I.'

He turned then and went to the barn

where Major, his horse, was just finishing another feed of stage-company oats. Malone scooped some more grain into the small sack he carried for spare fodder and secured the mouth with a string. His horse would have no time to graze on the thirty-mile plus journey that lay ahead.

He delayed a while, telling himself that the horse needed time to digest his fodder but secretly he hoped that Julie Crane might come to the barn to say goodbye. He pretended to be busy making last-minute adjustments to the pack to go behind the cantle and checking the horse's shoes, anything to delay leaving for a bit longer.

The bay horse was rested and, with plenty of oats inside him, was eager to go. He snorted and moved about as the scout cinched the saddle on his back and fastened the grain bag behind the cantle on top of a nosebag and a waterproof poncho. Taking a box of rimfire ammunition from his saddle-bag, he fully loaded his Winchester's magazine and slipped a few more rounds into the empty loops in his cartridge belt. Remembering that he had a dry route ahead, he led the horse to the trough and filled his water canteen from the well. He was just slipping his carbine into the loop on the saddle horn when Julie came out of the station.

'Don't forget,' she said, as he mounted, 'you will find us in Rocky Creek in about a week's time.'

He nodded and, for the first time, began to consider that he might just have been in the wrong line of work. He mounted but could find no other reason to delay. The other passengers were coming to the station door. 'I'll see you around,' he called to the group in general, then wheeled his mount and cantered over to have a last word with the sergeant before departing.

Nancy stood beside her sister-in-law and murmured, 'Despite what Tom says, that Jeff Malone might not be a bad catch.'

'Who says I want to catch him?'

Nancy laughed. 'You don't look too happy about seeing him go.'

If all went well, Malone calculated that he had six or seven hours of riding before he met the cavalry. He could do the journey in less time but wanted to keep his mount fit for service the next day.

It felt good to be away from walls and people and to be moving again, but the enjoyment was tempered by the thought that Grigg and his men had ridden off in the same direction. He would need to see them before they saw him. In the broken country ahead such a task would not always be easy.

5

An hour after leaving the stage station, Malone crossed the tracks left by the outlaws. They were riding directly north following the stage road while his course veered off to the north-east.

There was no mistaking the tracks. As one who often shod his own horses, he appreciated well-shaped hoofs and had admired the feet of the outlaw's black horse when he first saw it. Only the black horse could have made those perfectly shaped prints on the trail.

'As long as he keeps that horse, Grigg will be easy to track,' Malone said to his own mount. He had the habit of talking to his horses when travelling alone.

For hours he crossed barren, stony plains gouged by deep erosion, gullies with sparse vegetation and no running streams. No rider would come this way by choice but it was the shortest path to his rendezvous with the army. The blue line of hills to the north looked discouragingly distant and for a while he seemed to be making little progress but the bay horse steadily rolled the miles behind it. Sometimes walking, sometimes trotting and cantering where the ground was suitable, they gradually left the hard country. By mid-afternoon they could rest in the cool shade of cottonwoods, hackberrys and willows along a small creek. While the horse ate the oats, the scout chewed on a couple of strips of buffalo jerky that he carried in one saddle-bag for such occasions.

He knew that he was on the south fork of Sandy Creek. The north fork lay beyond the hills before him. The rising ground was covered with pines but these eventually gave way to scrubby oak and cedar. Loose shale and stones combined to make the footing difficult for a horse so he gave Major a good rest before continuing the journey. He could have followed the south fork to its junction with the north fork and ridden back along the other stream but the shortest route lay straight over the hills and that was the way he would go.

The climb was not an easy one but Major had been in worse country. He picked his way carefully over the loose footing and occasionally went up the steeper parts in a series of great, surging plunges while his rider left the reins loose and held the mane. He allowed the horse to pick its own way and the bay chose a zig-zag course up the steep slope.

Night was falling as he reached the crest of the range and was able to see across the undulating country on the other side. Before the light failed, he saw the stream's north fork clearly marked by the lighter green of willows and cottonwoods. Even as he paused to rest the horse after the climb, a light flared in the distance, then another.

'I reckon that's the army making camp for the night,' he said, as he patted Major's sweaty neck. 'Not far now, old pard.'

When he finally reached the camp he found Major Carter in fine spirits. His craggy, normally serious face was wreathed in smiles.

'You missed all the excitement, Jeff,' the officer greeted. 'We ran slap-bang into a big party of hostiles. They were careless and we were lucky to see them first. We got a few before they had time to scatter. We killed three and I think we wounded a few more. We should have got more but some of our new men don't shoot very well. Our horses were too worn out to chase them but I'll bet they didn't stop till they got back on the reservation. I've sent Captain Moller over to the agency with thirty men just to keep the scare into them. Of course, the Indian agent will swear that none of the Cheyenne have left the reservation so Moller will come away empty handed. But he might pick up a bit of useful information while he's there. I'm using this place as a base and am sending out patrols just in case the odd straggler is still loose around here.

They killed eight people on a south-bound coach and another two teamsters that they caught on the road. There might be others, too.'

'Luckily I was able to stop the north-bound coach, but things were pretty exciting there for a while,' Malone told him. 'We tangled with Jonas Grigg and his gang.'

The major was surprised by the scout's news and his face reflected his concern. 'What happened?' he asked eagerly. He had chased Grigg unsuccessfully at the end of the Civil War and knew that where the outlaw went, death and violence usually followed.

As Malone described the events at the stage station the officer's frown deepened. When the narration ended he said gravely, 'In your situation I would have done the same, but a lot of people are going to say that you should have shot Grigg and taken your chances with his gang. We have been chasing that devil for years. He started out in one of those guerrilla outfits during the Civil

War, but they were such criminals that the South disowned them all except for Moseby's men. Most of them never surrendered and have been outlaws ever since. Quantrill, Anderson, the James boys, the Youngers, they all came out of those guerrilla bands. They're mighty hard to catch and they still have a lot of friends who keep them well informed.'

'I agree with you there,' Malone told him. 'He seemed to have a good idea of how much money was in the coach's strongbox.'

'And you say that he's sworn to get you and this gambler fellow, Wilson?'

'That's right. I sat him on his ass and took his gun off him and he seemed to think it was personal.'

Carter chuckled. 'Not too many men have done that.'

'I'm not too worried about Grigg because I think he'll get out of this district as soon as he can. Living out so much with the army, I don't get to town all that often, so I'm not likely to strike him in my travels, but I am a bit worried about Wilson. I gave him Grigg's gun and he's wearing it around and showing it off. For a gambler, Wilson is not showing a lot of brains.'

'Take my advice, Jeff. You have made a very dangerous enemy who has to kill you to restore his reputation. Watch your back. From what I know of Grigg, he will find you when he wants you. He has a better intelligence system than a detective agency.'

'He wouldn't be all that far from here, Major. I cut his tracks this morning. While he's riding the horse he has at present, I can track him. If I could have a few troopers I could soon catch up with him.'

Carter shook his head. 'Unfortunately I can't let you go after him. We have been told to leave all outlaw chasing to the civilian authorities unless the criminals do something that directly involves the army. Also, the horses of this command are wearing down and are not up to chasing the sort of horses that outlaws usually ride. Now see to your horse and join me for dinner. It's only bacon, beans, hardtack and coffee I'm afraid.'

'It sure beats starving to death though.' Malone needed no reminder of just how hungry he was.

Nobody slept late in a cavalry camp and the soldiers were awake early, grooming and feeding their horses. Only when these tasks were finished and the horses saddled, did the troopers eat.

Carter, with Nelson and Quayle, his two lieutenants, was standing out on a piece of level ground staring intently at a distant mountain when Malone joined them after breakfast.

'What do you want me to do today, Major?'

The three officers were all wearing anxious expressions as they gazed at the mountain.

'Not a sign of them,' Carter said. Then, seeming to notice Malone for the first time, told him, 'I'll be with you in a second, Jeff.'

'Corporal Monson's a very experienced man,' Lieutenant Quayle said earnestly. 'He wouldn't miss reporting in.'

'Maybe the mirrors got broken or something like that,' Nelson suggested. He did not seem to be as concerned as his fellow officers. Nelson's hitch in the cavalry would soon be up and he had no intention of re-enlisting. He would soon be taking up a management job with a large freight line in Chicago.

Carter turned to Malone. 'I sent Corporal Monson and two men up to the top of that big mountain over there yesterday. They have a powerful telescope and a heliograph and lamps for signalling. They can see for miles from up there and if they spot any hostiles or even campfires they can direct a patrol to intercept them. We are trying to save our horses. They failed to report last night, but I thought that the darkness might have beaten them. Maybe the trees stopped them using the signal lamps. They should have reported by now though. I think something's wrong.'

Quayle was not long from West Point and looked the smartest of the trio in his new uniform. He was an ambitious young man and keen to make a big impression in his first year of active service. 'Do you think they might have struck Indian trouble, sir?'

'I doubt it. We combed that area thoroughly the day before yesterday. There's little horse feed or water over there and the Cheyenne would have no reason to go that way.' The major turned to Malone. 'What do you reckon, Jeff?'

'As I recall it, Major, the stage road runs just this side of that mountain. Grigg and his men were on that road yesterday. They might have had something to do with the problem.'

Carter shook his head. 'I doubt it. They always avoid getting involved with the military and there would not be much profit in robbing three soldiers. What else would they want from them?'

'They might have had a horse go lame,' Malone suggested, 'or they could be out of food and wanted your men's rations. Grigg and his friends were travelling mighty light when I saw them. What if I ride over there to take a look?'

Quayle was thirsting for action. 'That sounds like a good idea, sir. Could I take a squad along too?'

'Given the state of our horses, Mr Quayle, I would prefer to rest them as much as possible. Jeff's horse is the fittest one here.' Carter turned to the scout. 'I want you to see if you can find Monson and his men. If you locate them and all is well, get them to send a signal. If you need Mr Quayle and a squad of men, light a fire. I'll have men watching for signs from about noon. Any questions?'

'If I find that Grigg and his men are involved, do we go after them?'

'Not unless you actually see them in the area. I want to make that plain. We have neither the men nor the horses for chasing bandits. You are working for the army, Jeff, not the civilian law authorities. Our work in this campaign might not be over yet and we need you and all of our horses fit to travel.'

Malone was anxious as he left the camp. Somehow he felt that Grigg was involved in the disappearance of the soldiers. It was too much of a coincidence that the outlaws should be in the area at the same time. He felt frustrated too. The trail would still be hot and there was a good chance of tracking down the gang but he was restrained from doing so. He could see Carter's point of view but the prospect of destroying the Grigg gang was an attractive one. While the outlaw was at large he could always expect a bullet or worse.

He kept under as much cover as possible because he suspected that the missing soldiers had fallen foul of the gang. The thought of Grigg or one of his henchmen keeping watch through the powerful telescope did nothing for his peace of mind. The outlaw had sworn to kill him and seeing his enemy approaching alone would be a temptation hard to resist; that is, if Grigg even considered resisting such a thing. His reputation was that of a cold and vengeful killer.

Fortunately, much of the country he had to traverse was covered in pines and it was possible for the scout to escape observation for most of the journey. He chose a meandering route sticking to cover as much as possible even though it meant travelling extra distance. But he need not have taken the precaution because, a short while later, he realized that Grigg would not be observing from the mountain top.

It was the buzzards circling in the sky that gave him the first hint of the missing soldiers' fate. It was a sight he had often seen before and knew to be an ominous one. With a sense of foreboding, he urged the horse up the slope to the stage road that ran around the side of the mountain.

The tracks were there on the trail, those of several horses and a mule. They were at least a full day old. Among them Malone saw the perfectly shaped hoof prints of Grigg's black horse.

He heard the buzzards fighting among themselves before he rounded a bend in the trail and though he had a fair idea of what to expect, the sight still shocked him. Three soldiers were lying dead by the side of the trail. The buzzards took off when he appeared but they had already started work on the bodies. The bay horse shied at the scent of blood. Pools of it had dried around the corpses. Every man had a gaping wound across the throat and all had their hands tied behind them. A few yards away lay their mounts and the pack mule, also with their throats slashed. The men's pockets had been turned out, their weapons taken and the saddle-bags removed from their saddles.

The scene brought back the scout's

previous misgivings. He could not help wondering whether he should not have killed the outlaw while he had the chance. A nagging voice in his mind was telling him that he had made a bad decision in releasing Grigg.

Sickened and angered and plagued by self-doubt, Malone set the small signal fire on the trail to summon the party of troopers who would join him at the stage road.

6

By the time an eager Quayle and half-a-dozen not so eager troopers had reached the scene, Malone had read the signs and was reasonably sure of what had happened.

He explained to the horrified lieutenant what he had learned. 'These men met the Grigg gang on the trail. They probably had no reason to suspect them until it was too late and they found themselves at gunpoint. The gang took their weapons, ammunition, rations and blankets and loaded it all on to the spare horse they had. They did not want the army horses, they were too worn out. They could not let them go in case they headed back to the cavalry camp so they killed them. They killed the men in case they raised the alarm too soon and brought the army after them.'

'But why did they cut all their throats?' Quayle shuddered again at the thought.

'They knew that the rest of the force was close by and did not want to risk shots being heard.'

'And we call Indians savages. How much start do they have?' The young officer was angry now.

'Half a day at least and I've seen their horses. They haven't had weeks of campaigning like the cavalry horses. They're good ones and they're fresh and fit. We have no chance of catching them and it's against orders anyway.'

'They'll pay for this.'

'I reckon they will, Lieutenant, but I'm not sure when. Jonas Grigg has had a long run. I'd sure like to be around when they finally catch up with him though.'

They brought the bodies back to the camp and buried them that night. The anger among the soldiers was almost palpable and troopers complained openly about the lack of pursuit although the realists among them knew that such a course would be doomed to failure.

Malone was talking with the officers as they sat around a fire after the burials. Captain Moller and his detachment had rejoined the force while he was on the mountain. The captain's mission had yielded nothing of importance and the murders were still the main topic of conversation.

'I don't understand why they killed three men just for their weapons and rations,' Quayle said, as he aimlessly prodded the fire with a long stick.

Lieutenant Nelson turned up the collar of his overcoat against the early autumn chill and told him. 'They wouldn't need three revolvers and three Sharps .50 carbines but I think they knew where they could sell them. My guess is that they are short of cash and probably don't want to stir up the countryside by robbing a bank or a coach.'

'But I thought that outlaws had

plenty of money to throw about.'

The major had his say then. 'It costs outlaws a lot of money to keep clear of the law. They have to pay spies and sometimes bribe crooked law officers. They were probably planning the stage robbery that Jeff spoiled to give them a bankroll for a while. I haven't heard of the gang operating around these parts before so they might be a bit down on their luck.'

'But where would they sell the stolen weapons?' Quayle asked.

'I think I know where,' Malone said. 'There's a trading post on the Overland Trail run by a character named Ned Evans. He has long been suspected of selling stolen goods to wagon trains passing through and running guns and whiskey to the Indians. But so far nobody has caught him red-handed. Our Pawnee scouts have often picked up stories about Evans from other Indians. He's a slippery one.'

'I've heard of him from whispers around the Cheyenne agency too,'

Moller said, as he took a puff from his pipe.

'Wouldn't the Union Pacific take a lot of the passing trade that used to go on the old wagon road?' Nelson asked.

'It would, but there are plenty of people who cannot afford to move all their belongings by train. There are still enough wagons coming along to keep Evans in business, and by the time they get this far they need to replace worn teams, harness, even worn-out boots and clothing. They often buy more guns too. Indians don't like draft horses or mules and it has long been suspected that unwanted animals stolen in Indian raids are traded to Evans, too. Nobody has been able to prove anything against him, but you can bet that he would not hesitate to do business with Grigg and his men. If I was a lawman, that's where I would look first. Mind you, I have never been there, but from the comments of people who are paid to gather information, our friend Evans could be well worth a visit.'

Carter slowly filled his pipe and thought a while before he said, 'It goes against the grain not to pursue Grigg, but our horses are not up to the task.'

'You'll never get a better chance than this,' Malone reminded him. 'My horse is still fit.'

'I know that but I'm not sending you to get killed. One man can't do much and when that man is a special enemy of Grigg's, the idea is even less attractive.'

'But if we move quickly enough we might get on to him. The places where he can go are fairly limited and I know what he looks like. If the gang are down on their luck, they might be planning another crime before they leave the area. Chances are good that they will head for the trading post. We should strike while the iron is hot.'

Carter drew on his pipe for a second or two and turned to Quayle. 'Mister Quayle, tomorrow you will select eight men with suitable rations and a pack mule. The mounts are to be the fittest in the command. Captain Moller will select them. The men will travel light with no blankets or overcoats. They will rest tomorrow, but at dawn the day after you will take them north along the stage road. Your official mission is to look for signs that hostile warriors might have crossed the railroad and gone north to join the Sioux. Mister Malone will be waiting for you at the town of Blue Creek which is on the Overland Trail. You are to patrol along the trail in any direction that your scout thinks could lead to the apprehension of hostiles. If by chance, you should run into Jonas Grigg and his men you are to consider them hostile also. Do you understand?'

A smile of satisfaction flashed across the young lieutenant's face. 'I understand, sir, that I am looking for Cheyenne braves who have left the reservation, but if we accidentally run into Jonas Grigg we should take appropriate action.'

'That's correct.'

Carter turned to the scout. 'You can start in the morning if you feel that your horse is up to it. Get on Grigg's tracks and leave a clear trail for Mr Quayle to follow. I am taking the rest of the command back to Fort Morgan. The Cheyenne don't raid in winter so we have finished this campaign. Quayle can keep in touch with me by telegraph for orders. Does that plan suit you? Let me know if you see any problems.'

'I can't see anything wrong with that idea at all. My horse is fine. He cost me a lot of money when I bought him but he's worth every cent. I'll start first thing in the morning and wait for the lieutenant at Blue Creek. As I understand things, he is to check at any trading posts to determine if the traders have any intelligence regarding the movement of Indian bands and who knows ... maybe this Evans has something to tell us.'

'We seem to understand each other perfectly.'

Those few casual instructions were

what Malone had been hoping to hear. They left Quayle with the option of chasing the outlaws while openly conducting military business.

'There's another thing,' the major told him. 'Your work with us would normally terminate when we get back to Fort Morgan for winter quarters, but you can stay on the payroll as long as Mr Quayle needs you. Does that suit you?'

'It sure does, a bit of extra cash will not go amiss if there's a long winter.'

Malone slept restlessly that night. He was eager to be on the bandits' trail. He felt that their start had already been too long delayed and begrudged every minute he was forced to wait in camp. Carefully he compared notes with Quayle arranging a system of signals to leave on the trail to give the soldiers an idea of his whereabouts.

By sunrise the next day he was on his way. The tracks were easy to find as no other traffic had been along the coach road. As he had promised Quayle, at the few forks he encountered, he left a small cairn of stones in the middle of the trail as an indication of the path he had taken.

The hoofprints were deep and wide apart, clear evidence that Grigg and his henchmen wanted to be well clear of the murder scene as quickly as possible. The tracks led past a burned-out stage station, its eerie, blackened ruins and three fresh graves giving mute testimony as to the ferocity of the last Indian outbreak. Malone did not know whether the victims had been stage passengers or company staff, but he gave them little thought. His mind was centred on the men somewhere ahead. The outlaws had stopped and looked around but the scout had no such curiosity. Every second that Grigg's men delayed brought him closer to them.

He found where they had camped for the night but pressed on for another hour to gain a bit more ground on his quarry. Because he carried a supply of oats for his horse he could tether it close to where he slept and it could eat without having to wander about and graze. He lit no fire and concealed his mount and himself in the brush a short distance from the trail. Through sheer force of habit he selected a place where any chance passers-by were unlikely to see him.

The first red streaks of dawn were showing in the eastern sky as he saddled up again and munched a piece of army hardtack that substituted for breakfast. The biscuit was hard, not particularly tasty and it required good teeth to chew even after he had broken it with his rifle butt, but by eating as he rode, he gained time.

The tracks showed that Grigg and his men were travelling slower. They were also having trouble with the improvised pack. Dakota's riding saddle was not designed for packing and his horse had almost no wither. It was difficult to keep the load evenly balanced and the saddle tended to slip to one side or the other.

'That pack's slipping,' Malone told his horse. 'That's the second time they've stopped to straighten it. We're gaining on them, Major, old pard.'

He curbed his impatience and gave Major an hour's rest and grazing when they found a patch of good grass and a small creek trickling nearby. The outlaws had also stopped there. Footprints showed in the mud at the creek's edge. One print was clear and well defined from a boot that was fairly new. He guessed that he was looking at the track of Clem Ryan, the dandy of the gang.

Then, just when the scout was sure that the outlaws were headed for Blue Creek, their tracks veered off the stage road and into rolling sage-covered country to the north-east. He realized then that tracking had been too easy. Grigg was now going to make himself hard to find. The trail through the sage would be hard to follow and the cavalry arriving the next day would find it even harder.

Malone knew that Blue Creek and the Overland Trail lay only a few miles farther along the trail so he left a small cairn indicating that he had gone in that direction. He would continue on the gang's trail and hoped to rendezvous with the soldiers in Blue Creek the following day. He was sure that Grigg and his men would rest and resupply themselves somewhere in the area. If they did not he was in trouble. He would have lost the gang and would have committed a most serious crime for an army scout, that of sending the troops in the wrong direction.

7

'That damn pack is slippin' again,' Winchell called to the rest of the gang who were riding ahead of him. 'Hold up awhile till I fix it.'

'Leave it as it is. We're nearly at the trading post,' Grigg commanded.

'But it will cause a sore back,' Winchell protested.

'Dakota won't be needing that horse again and neither will we,' Ryan told him.

'We'd get more for it from Evans without a sore back.'

'Stop arguing, Earl. Time's more important than horses,' Grigg said angrily. 'Do you want the army to catch up with us?'

★   ★   ★

Malone found tracking through the sage reasonably easy. Some of the low shrubs were bent or broken and between the plants the hoof marks showed plainly on the bare red earth. But conditions would change when night fell. Topping a ridge he suddenly saw a broad stream running through the shallow valley below. Though he had not been there before, he knew from army maps that it was Blue Creek. The name was a misnomer because the water was muddy brown. The tracks of the riders led into the creek but none showed on the opposite bank. They had ridden along the streambed to hide their trail.

'In some country that trick works,' the scout told his horse, 'but there's a lot of clay in these creeks, so they're not as smart as they think.'

Dismounting, the scout felt around in the shallow, muddy water. He could not see it but he soon found what he sought, the print of a hoof deeply embedded in the clay. It was pointed upstream. He led the horse a short distance along the stream to a narrow point and felt around again just to be sure that the animal had not changed direction. The water was a little deeper and this time he wet his shirtsleeve to the elbow, but again he found another impression in the clay.

He glanced at the sun lowering in the west as he remounted. His most pressing need then was to find where the gang had left the water before the light failed.

* * *

Ned Evans was tying a bundle of Indian-tanned buckskin together when he heard the horses approaching. He was a small untidy man with long black hair and a beard. His wire-framed spectacles proved a strange contrast to the man's dark features. The pale-grey eyes behind the glasses were furtive and suspicious. 'Charlie,' he yelled. 'Riders comin'.'

Charlie, his massive part-Cherokee assistant picked up a double-barrelled gun and took up a position at a door from where he could cover activities in the trading area.

Evans tucked a small .38 in the back of his belt and walked to the building's entrance. 'It's Jonas,' he said, in a relieved tone. 'Light the lamps. Looks like we have a bit of business.'

Grigg's party halted in front of the buildings.

'Howdy, Ned,' the leader said, as he dismounted. He shook hands and introduced the rest of the gang.

'What can I do for you, Jonas?'

'Seen any lawmen around?'

'Not for weeks. You know they ain't interested in an honest trader like me. Now what brings you to these parts?'

'I have a bit of trading to do. In return I want food and rest for my men and horses for a couple of days. I have a good horse, a saddle and bridle, three .44 Colt Armies, three Sharps .50 carbines and a supply of ammunition for both types.'

Evans looked at him sharply. 'Sounds

like army stuff. You ain't got the army after you?'

'They aren't after me,' Grigg lied. 'Nobody will ask you awkward questions because if I know you, these guns will go to the Indians. Anyone who finds them later will reckon they got them from dead soldiers.'

The trader made no denial. Instead he asked, 'What about the horse?'

'The horse is a good one but his withers could be a mite rubbed. But you'll see it when the saddle's off. Most likely it's nothing that a week's rest won't fix. I can give you a legal bill of sale for it that will stand up anywhere.'

Evans smiled sensing that the deal could prove profitable for him. He was secretly relieved that the outlaw was prepared to deal for he knew that he could just as easily take what he wanted at gunpoint. 'Put your horses in the corral,' he told them, 'then come into the trading post. I'll open a jug and we'll talk business. I take it that whatever business matter you were on did not go as planned, as one of your men ain't with you although his horse is.'

'You're right, Ned. But the less you know about it the better,' Grigg muttered. 'Now let's see if your whiskey has improved.'

⋆   ⋆   ⋆

Malone found where the gang had left the creek and then the light failed. He was sitting on his horse looking about when a lighted window suddenly showed in the distance. Cautiously he rode toward it. Suddenly the bay horse stepped on to a well-worn trail that led to a dimly seen group of buildings about a quarter of a mile away. Though he had never been there, he suspected that it was Evans's trading post.

He dismounted and hitched his horse in a clump of pines. Satisfied that it could not be seen, he stole forward quietly on foot. He stayed in the shadows at the edge of the trail halting occasionally to observe and listen. A man with as many secrets as Evans was reputed to have might well have a guard along the trail. Soon he could discern a main building with a sign in front, a couple of ramshackle sheds and two large corrals. Horses moved restlessly in one corral.

Suddenly a dog barked and the scout cursed silently. He was unsure if it had caught his scent but to go closer was to risk being discovered. Malone sank to the ground as silently as he could.

A door opened and a big man was framed in the doorway by the light behind him. Fortunately the man paid no attention to the barking dog except to swear at it and tell it to be silent. He went to the corral and re-emerged leading five horses. They were unsaddled but as they passed the pool of light thrown through the open door, the scout thought that he recognized Grigg's black animal. Certainly they were not the mustang types usually ridden by citizens in that locality.

Deciding against pushing his luck and frightening his quarry, Malone crept quietly to his horse and rode back along the trail. A mile further along it he met a well-used wagon road. By the deep ruts worn by thousands of wheels, he knew he was at the Overland Trail. He turned west along it and an hour later sighted the lights of Blue Creek.

The town was small, just a single street and a few buildings. A couple of horses were hitched to the rail in front of the only saloon. He found a livery stable adjacent to the hotel so when his horse and he were both accommodated he treated himself to a large steak dinner in the hotel dining-room. He would have preferred a bath and a shave before eating, but the cook was anxious to close the kitchen so he made the meal his first priority.

The bed felt strangely soft after so many nights of sleeping on the ground but eventually he fell asleep. A couple of times he awoke wondering where he was and was reaching for his revolver but the soft bed told him that all was well and he sank back secure in the knowledge that vigilance was no longer necessary.

Next morning after a hearty breakfast of bacon and eggs and coffee, he checked again on his horse while waiting for the general store to open. The stablehand was cleaning out the stalls but seemed happy to stop and talk.

'Where did you get that good horse?' he asked Malone. 'Looks like a Kentucky thoroughbred to me.'

'He is. He belonged to a cavalry major who was retiring and he gave me first offer. The horse had been out here long enough to be fully acclimatized and I reckoned it was money well spent. He cost me the price of two ordinary horses but has outlasted any three I could buy out here.'

The stablehand nodded in agreement. 'You get folks claiming that mustangs are better, but I always found that well-bred horses last best if they are looked after.'

'You're right there,' Malone agreed. 'Even the American horses that the army use give better service after the first year. It takes them about a year to acclimatize because they are nearly all raised on farms in the East, but once they get used to the seasons here, they can take a lot of work. The weight and travelling wear them down on long campaigns but the same treatment would kill mustangs. Do you see many good horses come through here?'

The man leaned on his pitchfork and rubbed his stubbled chin. 'About a week ago five men stayed overnight. They all had good horses but one black one was a real beauty, a bit after the style of yours.'

Trying to conceal his interest, Malone asked casually, 'It's unusual to see so many good horses at one time. What line of work were the riders in? Were they cattlemen, or lawmen, or just wealthy Eastern dudes?'

The man looked about nervously as though he feared being overheard. 'My guess is that they were gunmen of some kind, probably dodging the law. They had enough artillery to start a war and they didn't stay long. That sort are usually looking for Evans's trading post a few miles out of town, but these didn't say anything about it, at least that I heard. I was glad to see them leave town though. We don't have a law officer here and they looked bad *hombres* to get on the wrong side of.'

'Looks like you don't have to worry now. They've probably moved on.'

'One of 'em has. I saw him gettin' on the south-bound stage a few days ago. He was cleaned up and only packin' one gun, but his pards still looked the same. Ain't seen the rest of 'em back in town since, so they probably are gone but I ain't sorry. They were a bad-lookin' bunch.'

'I was thinking of getting a pack-saddle and maybe an Indian pony to carry it. Do you reckon I'd have any luck with this Evans?'

'I'm pretty sure he'd have what you need, but he might try to charge too much. He's a greedy sonofabitch. He trades a few ponies with the Cheyenne from the reservation so they should be safe enough to buy, but I'd be suspicious of where he got some of the mules and harness horses that he trades to folks on the trail.'

Leaving the stables, Malone found that the general store was open so he bought himself a couple of new shirts and returned to his hotel room to change. He had just finished dressing when he heard a horse in the street and looked out the window. A rider was passing on a spotted Indian pony. Something familiar caught the scout's eye. His view was angled so that he could not see the rider's face, but he recognized the black hat with the white horsehair band. He had last seen it on Clem Ryan at the stage station.

The scout ran from his room in time to see the rider dismount about fifty yards up the street at the saloon. He stepped out on to the boardwalk and casually strolled a bit closer. The stranger was about to enter the building when he glanced back and saw Malone who at the same time found himself looking at Clem Ryan.

Both men reacted automatically.

The outlaw's hands fairly flew to his guns and they came out of their holsters before the scout's weapon cleared leather. The first shot sang past Malone's ear viciously. The second shot missed by another narrow margin, but by then the scout had sent off his first carefully aimed shot. The .44 slug hit Ryan in the upper body causing him to reel and drop one gun. He fired one more hasty shot. Again his aim was astray.

Malone sighted carefully and his second shot knocked the gunman off his feet. 'Drop your gun, Ryan,' he commanded.

Painfully the outlaw struggled to his knees, tried to lift his gun and as if finding the weight beyond him, fell forward again on his face.

The first onlooker to reach the scene was the man from the livery stable. As Malone kicked the gun from Ryan's hand and bent to turn him over, the man said, 'You got him. That was one of them hardcases I was tellin' you about.'

A cowboy from the saloon joined them. 'I thought he had you,' he told Malone. 'That was the fastest draw I ever saw. He beat you to the shot twice.'

'I never saw a fast-draw man yet who could shoot straight over a bit of distance,' the scout told him. 'If I'd been a bit closer I might not be talking to you now. He didn't miss by much.' He felt for a pulse, found none and straightened up. 'He's stone dead.'

A thin, grey-haired man pushed through the small crowd that was gathering. 'I'm John Pascoe, a Justice of the Peace. What happened?'

'That *hombre* just tried to kill Mr Malone,' the livery-man said excitedly.

'I saw it all. He fired two shots before Malone even fired one.'

'I'm Jeff Malone, an army scout. I believe that man is an outlaw named Clem Ryan who was involved in the murder of three soldiers a couple of days ago.'

The justice said. 'I haven't heard of any soldiers being murdered lately.'

'You'll hear about it today,' Malone said. 'There's an officer and a squad of men on the way. Now, as a Justice of the Peace, do you want to search this man, or will I?'

8

With Pascoe looking on, Malone went through Ryan's pockets. He found a small revolver in a shoulder holster, eight dollars in change and cigarette makings but nothing to identify positively the man he had shot. A search of the saddle-bags on the pony yielded a box with a few Henry rifle cartridges but little else.

'He must have come to town to buy something,' Pascoe said. 'That would be why the saddle-bags are empty — must be staying around here somewhere.'

'Looks that way,' Malone agreed. He knew where the outlaw was staying but did not want to disclose too much until the soldiers arrived. It appeared that Ryan was resting his own horse and had borrowed the pony from Evans.

Pascoe took over the corpse and the

dead man's possessions. He noted statements from various witnesses. 'I'll need to send a report to the county sheriff,' he explained. 'There is no need to worry, Mr Malone, and if the man is the outlaw we think he is, you might find yourself in receipt of a large reward. This could be your lucky day.'

'It already has been, another few paces closer and it would most likely have been me lying there. He was very fast getting those guns out.'

After giving his address as care of the army at Fort Morgan, Malone left the group and hurried to the livery stable. The stablehand was still excited by the drama he had seen.

'I never saw shootin' like that, Mr Malone. You never missed a shot.'

'That's because I took the time to aim. But there was a lot of luck involved, I'm no gunfighter . . . and my name's Jeff. I want to ask you a favour.'

'Just name it.'

'I think you and I both know where the late Mr Ryan came from. Don't say anything to anyone. We don't want the rest of the gang being warned. There are some soldiers due here today and when they arrive, we will pay the others a visit. I'd appreciate it, too, if you would have my horse ready to go at short notice. What do I owe you?'

'My name's Henry . . . Henry Adams. I reckon two dollars fifty will settle your bill.'

The scout fished three dollars from his pocket. 'That's close enough for me, Henry. Remember now, not a word about where Ryan came from. I'm going to settle my hotel bill and be ready to move.'

As the soldiers had not arrived, Malone waited in the town's only restaurant. He ordered coffee and cake and bought a small sack of freshly made biscuits to put in his saddle-bag. There was no guarantee that he would be eating at regular times for the remainder of the day.

Just before noon, Quayle and his troopers arrived. An impatient Malone, already holding his horse's reins, met them in the street.

'You made good time, Lieutenant. It's best though that you don't dismount. Grigg's gang are at Ned Evans's trading post a couple of miles from here. We need to get there as quick as we can. I'll explain as we go.'

★ ★ ★

Jonas Grigg was pacing the floor in the trading-post kitchen. 'I tell you, Ned, something's wrong. Clem should be back by now. He only went to town to get a decent bottle of whiskey.'

'Maybe he stayed a while in the saloon to sample it. There was no need to go at all. I have a whole barrel of whiskey here. Your men are just too fussy, Jonas.'

Grigg was not interested in the dubious merits of the whiskey that Evans sold to the Indians. He knew that Ryan was not a heavy drinker. His brow furrowed as he walked out to the corral and looked towards town. None of the horses was saddled, a situation that only added to his unease.

Wilkes and Winchell were playing cards inside the trading post and he was about to join them when something above the trees in the middle distance caught his eye. A dust cloud was rising, the type stirred up by horses. A sixth sense warned the outlaw that trouble was approaching.

With instincts honed by years of being hunted, Grigg reacted swiftly. He ran to the corral, caught the closest horse, slipped a bridle on it and vaulted on to its bare back after opening the corral gate.

Wilkes and Winchell heard the horse gallop away and looked up from their cards.

'Something's wrong,' Winchell muttered in alarm. 'I think I just saw Jonas ride by the window.'

Wilkes swore and ran to the front of the building to look out of the windows. 'There's riders comin'. Jonas has left us behind. Get to the corral quick.'

The trampling of horses came nearer as the two outlaws ran to the corral but Grigg had left open the gate and their horses had escaped.

Evans and Charlie came hurrying from one of the sheds.

'Get out of here,' the trader yelled. 'There's soldiers comin'. You can't get caught here. Get up that hill at the back and hide in the brush.'

Both men snatched up their carbines and ran from the building hoping to reach the brush before the soldiers saw them. They were too late.

Quayle pointed as the horsemen neared the post. 'They are trying to get away. I just saw them running into that clump of trees. They aren't at the trading post. They're over there in that patch of trees.'

'There could be some in the trading post,' Malone warned, but the lieutenant had thrown caution to the winds.

'Form a skirmish line,' he shouted, and the soldiers fanned out into a single

112

line abreast. 'Follow me!'

The lieutenant had found the excitement he sought and led his small army forward at the gallop.

Two repeating rifles opened up from the trees. The first couple of shots missed, but then as the horsemen closed the distance, one of the soldiers' horses came down in a crashing somersault flinging the rider out ahead of it. Another soldier sagged over his horse's neck and clung to the mane.

Malone was on the flank of the charging line. He saw clouds of gunsmoke betraying the presence of the riflemen and rode straight at them.

A couple of horse lengths short of the trees, Quayle's chestnut horse reared high and toppled backwards but there was no stopping the rush. Ignoring their fallen leader, the troopers spurred into the trees.

All was noise, the smashing of timber, reports of rifles and revolvers and shouts of excited men. Powder-smoke hung in a cloud around the battleground hindering visibility for friend and foe equally.

Malone kept clear of the mêlée watching in case one of the outlaws made a break. There was a real chance of being shot by his own side in the confusion among the trees and he had no intention of going in there unless it became necessary.

'I surrender!' a man screamed. 'Don't shoot!'

Quayle was on his feet brandishing his revolver. 'Cease firing,' he bawled.

A second later, the guns fell silent.

'I'm comin' out,' Wilkes called. 'Don't shoot.'

'What about the others?' Quayle demanded.

'There was only Earl an' me. He's dead . . . shot to bits.'

'Come out, but don't make any wrong moves,' the officer warned.

Wilkes had a broken arm dangling at his side and held the other one up as he emerged from cover.

'Where's Grigg?' Malone demanded.

'Gone . . . run out on us . . . didn't even give us a warnin'.'

'What are our casualties, Corporal?' Quayle looked a little pale and shaken but still very much in control.

'Trooper Musgrove's dead, sir. Trooper Baum has a bullet in his leg. We had two horses killed and we got one wounded.'

'See what you can do for Baum. 'You' — Quayle pointed to Wilkes — 'come over here.'

'Just before you do,' Malone said, as he dismounted. Reaching behind the prisoner he extracted a Bowie knife from a beaded scabbard on the man's gunbelt. Holding up the weapon he said to the lieutenant, 'I think we have just found the one who cut those soldiers' throats the other day.'

'I didn't do it,' the prisoner protested. 'Jonas did it. He borrowed my knife.'

Anger flared in Quayle's eyes but he quickly regained control. 'I'm tempted to shoot you right here, but I might enjoy it better if I see you hang. Now we'll get back to the trading post. There are wounds to be tended and I think Ned Evans has some explaining to do.'

'Which way did Griggs go?' Malone demanded from the prisoner.

'I don't know. That's the truth. He run out on us.'

'Don't worry about him, Malone; I think we should be questioning Evans now. We don't want him getting away, too.' As he spoke, the lieutenant picked up the hat that had fallen from his head when his mount was killed. His face froze as he beheld a bullet hole through the crown. Then he jammed the hat on his head and borrowed a trooper's mount. He ordered three nearby soldiers to follow him and left the others to care for the wounded and guard the prisoner. 'That man you are guarding is not to come to any harm,' he warned. 'He will not be shot while trying to escape. I'll court-martial anyone who tries a trick like that.'

They rode back to the trading post.

The door was open but there was no sign of the owner.

'Come out here, Evans,' Quayle called. 'If we have to come in after you, we're coming in shooting.'

Evans put his head around the door cautiously. 'What do you want?'

'I want to know why a gang of outlaws has been staying here.'

'I didn't know they were outlaws. They were strangers to me. They just came to do a bit of trading.'

'And you just showed them a bit of hospitality for the night,' Quayle said sarcastically.

'That's right. That's all it was, just hospitality. I was trying to do a deal for their horses. We don't see many like them in these parts.'

'We're coming in, Evans. Don't do anything silly, or we'll shoot.'

'Hell, Lieutenant, I ain't got nothin' to hide. You won't have any trouble from me.' The trader knew this was no time to try bucking the odds.

They dismounted and entered the

gloomy cavernous room where Evans conducted most of his business. Goods of all sorts were stacked on shelves, in corners and even hanging from the rafters.

Quayle stood with his hands on his hips and took in the room.

Evans had regained some of his composure and asked, 'Do you want to buy the whole place, Lieutenant, or are you interested in something particular?'

'I'm just wondering where to start taking this rat's nest apart.'

'Maybe I can help. Tell me what interests you first.'

'What firearms are you selling?'

Evans pointed. 'Over there in the rack behind the counter. What are you looking for particularly?'

The officer ordered a trooper, 'See if you can find three Sharps carbines and army-issue Colt revolvers.'

The trader said casually, 'I have a few. Thousands of both types of arms were sold after the Civil War, half the folks moving west were armed with them. A lot have been traded through here.'

A soldier indicated three military carbines standing side by side in a rack. 'These look familiar, Lieutenant.'

All three weapons had been well cared for in contrast to some of the neglected rifles in the same rack.

'Civil-war weapons,' Evans said dismissively. 'There are thousands about.'

Quayle picked up one of the carbines and depressed the trigger guard so that the breech opened. 'That's where you're wrong, Evans. During the war these carbines were .52 calibre and fired the old linen cartridge. After the war the government had them re-barrelled and had firing pins fitted to take the .50 calibre metallic cartridge. They were reissued when the Spencer carbines were ruled obsolete and were recalled. I am going to have the serial numbers of these carbines checked, and if I find they came from this regiment, you are in serious trouble.'

119

'I didn't know where they got them . . . honest.'

Two military nosebags hanging on the wall caught the scout's eye. He looked inside one. There were a few loose paper cartridges, and several little rectangular brown cardboard boxes. He recalled that the murdered soldiers had been robbed of their ammunition but the pouches were left on their belts. Paper cartridges were easy to damage and until they were needed, most soldiers kept them in lots of six in the small boxes in which they came from the factory. To prevent damage, the looters had carried the ammunition in the canvas nosebag. The second bag contained brass-cased carbine ammunition, some in boxes of ten and other cartridges loose.

'I've just found the ammunition that was taken the other day,' Malone announced. 'I reckon the three Colts are also here somewhere.'

'Here they are,' called a trooper, who

had been checking a box of assorted handguns.

Within minutes, the searchers found the blankets and saddle-bags that the outlaws had also taken.

Quayle walked to where Evans was nervously sitting on a box in the corner of the room. 'I'm arresting you, Evans, for having stolen government property in your possession.'

'You can't do that. I'm an honest trader. I didn't know the stuff was stolen. People bring all sortsa stuff to trade all the time.'

'We have one of your late guests still alive. I intend to question him at length and if he incriminates you in the murder of those soldiers, I'll see to it that you hang.'

Malone took a walk outside the post and looked around. He saw Grigg's footprints at the corral gate and noted that he had taken a different horse. Tracking the fugitive would be much harder now.

9

Grigg fled eastward along the Overland Trail. He paused long enough to murder a traveller for his saddle and pack horse and by the time he reached Kansas he was fully outfitted again. He turned north then into Nebraska territory. In Omaha he renewed his acquaintance with Lou Williams.

Williams was working as a faro dealer in a saloon. None suspected that the pleasant gambler they knew as Bill Lewis was a former Missouri guerrilla with a bloody reputation.

For a criminal, Williams had much going for him. He looked so ordinary and everyday that people could point to men like him in every town. He never drew attention to himself in looks or manner. Only his victims remembered the cold-eyed, ruthless killer, but not many of them were living.

Grigg had deliberately assumed a scruffy, unkempt look like a man down on his luck looking for whatever work would pick up a few dollars. At first, Williams did not recognize him when he approached the faro table. 'Think well before you buck the tiger here, my friend. This game could be a bit rich for your blood.'

'I think I could handle it, Lou.'

'Jonas . . . what are you doing here?'

'Looking for an old riding pal, Lou. I'm staying at the Palace Hotel. It doesn't exactly fit its name but it suits me at present. What time do you finish work?'

'About midnight unless someone really starts betting heavily.'

'I'll wait up for you. I'm in room twelve. Bring a bottle. I have a proposal that might interest you.'

'Hell, Jonas, I thought you'd be dead by now. I read in a newspaper weeks ago, that your outfit was all busted up and the law was expecting to catch up with you any day.'

123

'Don't believe all you read in the papers, Lou. I'm recruiting good men this time. I'll see you tonight.'

Williams had not been making much money as a gambler, but he was beginning to enjoy a quieter life inside the law. He was tempted to refuse Grigg's offer but old loyalty and the lure of easy money called him again. After much deliberation he decided that one more job with Grigg would be to his advantage.

* * *

Winter had set in. The Indians were remaining on the reservations and until spring, Malone was out of a job. He had saved his earnings and would have enough money to see him through until the army came out of winter quarters in early spring. With a newly purchased mule to carry his few belongings, he pointed Major towards the town of Rocky Creek a hundred miles to the north.

He told himself that Julie Crane would not remember him, or would already be engaged to some townsman with a respectable job and might no longer want to know him, but he had nothing better to do. He had never been to Rocky Creek so it would be somewhere new.

The journey was long and cold. Sleet was falling as the light failed and he was very glad to see the town after three days on the trail.

The town was bigger than he thought it would be although the weather was keeping people off the streets. He found a livery stable and arranged to get his animals and outfit under cover.

The livery-man turned out to be a former farrier-sergeant named Mike Hemings, an old friend from his early times with the army.

'It's good to see you, Jeff,' Hemings said, as he shook his hand. 'What brings you up this way?'

'Just looking at new places, Mike. I thought I'd stop here a while and let

Major get a bit of a rest. He's had a lot of work lately.'

'He still looks good though, Jeff. I'll give him the royal treatment while he's here. Where are you staying?'

'I hadn't figured that far ahead. Do you know of any cabins that might be for rent?'

Hemings stroked his thick, black beard for a second. 'You might be in luck. There were a few cabins built for railroad people when they were putting the line through. Some of them are sure to be empty. Sam Lauder, the lawyer, has charge of them and I'm pretty sure you could rent one. But his office is shut now. Camp here for the night. It's warm and dry. I'd invite you around to my place but it's mighty small with Rose and me and the three kids.'

'So you married that red-haired girl you were so keen on?'

'Sure did. It was the best thing I ever done . . . It's funny you turning up now, I heard about you from a lady, only the other day.'

126

Malone forgot his weariness. 'Who was telling you about me?'

'A lady named Julie Crane. See that grey pony in the end stall? It's hers. She was telling me how you laid out Jonas Grigg with one punch and let daylight through a whole passel of outlaws.'

'I think she might have got carried away a bit. I did knock Grigg down, but to save our skins I had to let him go. I'm not sure it was all that smart as he has sworn to kill me.'

'That might not be so easy, Jeff. I read where you killed Clem Ryan in a shoot-out and he was mighty fast with a gun.'

'I was lucky. As you well know, the six-shooter is not exactly a precision instrument when drawn quickly and fired from the hip. You need to aim carefully. Fast draws only work when the shooter and the target are close together. As luck would have it the range was a bit too long for Ryan's brand of shooting.'

'I seem to recall you were pretty

handy with horses. How would you feel about breaking in a couple of young ones for me?'

Malone thought a while before replying. 'Tell me about them.'

'They're a pair of geldings I bought cheap when a rancher here sold up. They have been taught to lead and tie up but I don't have the time to keep them in regular riding. The buckskin one might pitch a bit on his first ride but the chestnut seems very quiet. Both have the makings of good, useful horses.'

'This time of year is not the best for breaking broncs. The wind often spooks them and some buck to keep warm. But they would give me something to ride about on while Major's resting. My Hope saddle is a bit light for the job though. Do you have a good stock saddle I could borrow?'

'That's no problem. I have a good double-rigged saddle that I bought off a Texas trail-herder who ran short of cash. You can borrow that while you are here. You can have the usual bronc buster's pay of three dollars a head or some other deal if it suits you better.'

'What if I do the job for nothing, but you supply feed for my horse and mule?'

'Good. Tonight you come home to dinner with me and tomorrow we see Lauder about renting a cabin for you. I have a couple of good corrals behind this barn and the two horses are there. It's a bit dark now so we won't go out there. You can see them better in the morning.'

'I'm getting to like this town already,' Malone laughed. Then, trying to sound casual, he remarked, 'I thought Julie Crane would have been engaged or married by now.'

'No, she's still unattached although half the single men for miles around are trying to win her heart. There's a gambler named Wilson who works at the Gilded Lily saloon who reckons he will win her over. But I don't like his chances.'

'Is he a smart-looking fellow, about thirty, with brown curly hair and a moustache?'

'That sounds like him. Do you know him?'

'He was a passenger on the coach when we tangled with Jonas Grigg. Does he still have Grigg's gun?'

'Sure has, he's always showing it around. Most folks don't believe him. They think it's all a story. He's supposed to be a nice guy, but a bit empty-headed. Nobody knows when he's serious and when he's not.'

Malone frowned. 'He's a fool. Grigg has sworn to kill him. I told him to get rid of that gun and to keep out of sight. If the stories are right about Grigg's spies, he'll soon find out where he is. He's gambling that the law will catch up with Grigg first. But I'm not sure that will happen.'

'I think Grigg's run is coming to an end, Jeff. His gang's scattered, or dead, or in the calaboose. He won't last much longer.'

'I'm not so sure. There are always plenty of no-goods who will take up with him if they get the chance. He seems to have had a charmed life to date. Some might want to join him because he seems so lucky, although that luck doesn't always extend to his men. He ran out on the last couple, saw trouble coming and didn't wait around to warn them.'

'Right now, he's the least of my worries. He's hardly likely to rob a livery stable. I'll just make sure that all the horses are right and then we'll head home for dinner. Rose will be pleased to see you.'

The next couple of hours passed pleasantly with Hemings and his family, but weariness from his long ride was setting in and aware that his friend started work early, Malone stood up and stretched.

'I'm sorry to break up the party, folks but I reckon I need my beauty sleep. Thank you, Rose. It's been a good night and I enjoyed that meal.'

'It was only stew,' Rose laughed.

'I know, but it was stew that I didn't cook myself and it always tastes better when someone else has cooked it.'

Hemings produced a large key. 'This opens the padlock on the back door of the stables. Make yourself comfortable and I'll bring breakfast around in the morning.'

Malone pocketed the key, said good night and strolled back along the main street to the stables. The lights were still on at the Gilded Lily saloon and he looked over the batwing doors as he passed. There were a couple of drinkers at tables and he recognized Wilson deeply engrossed in a card game at the far end of the room. He debated going in for a quick drink but decided that sleep would be more beneficial. He was about to turn away when a man came to the doors and pushed through.

The man's face was vaguely familiar. He gave no indication that he knew Malone, but the scout was sure that he knew him from somewhere. The

132

stranger's nose had been badly broken and there was a scar on his left cheek that a week's growth of beard did not disguise. He was locking the stable door behind himself when he remembered the man's name. He was Frank Rydell who had briefly worked as a mule packer for the army. Malone remembered the day a young mule had kicked the packer in the face. He remembered hearing later that Rydell was in trouble over pilfered army supplies, but had been out with a patrol when the packer's theft was discovered. He knew none of the details about the incident and had almost forgotten the man.

But Rydell had not forgotten Malone although he pretended not to recognize him. The word had been out for some time among those who lived on the fringes of the law: Jonas Grigg would pay big money to the man who would supply him with information regarding the whereabouts of two men he had sworn to kill. The former packer thought he had struck the jackpot when he recognized Wilson, but now it was a double jackpot. Malone was also in the same town.

Rydell knew exactly where to go to turn his information into cash. A shyster lawyer in Denver was the man who had advised of the reward. Zack Gilmore had been a silent partner of Jonas Grigg for several years and collected intelligence for the outlaw. Through a network of small-time criminals, he picked up snippets of information and guided Grigg to hit the more lucrative banks and gold shipments.

As he made his way to the cabin he was renting, Rydell began fishing change from his pocket. He needed to be sure that he could pay for the telegraph he would send in the morning.

Fortune, it seemed, was smiling on him at last.

10

Malone was awake and fully dressed when Hemings arrived with his breakfast on a tray covered by a clean dish towel.

'I was just going to start cleaning out the stalls.'

'Don't worry about that,' Hemings told him. 'Eat your breakfast while it's hot and then go and see Lauder about a cabin. You don't want to be going down there covered in straw and horse manure. Take your time coming back. There won't be much happening today. Call in and see some of your friends while you still look respectable.'

'I might just do that. I don't look respectable all that often.'

Sam Lauder was a plump, middle-aged man, his grey hair neatly combed and his suit clean and carefully pressed. A heavy gold watch chain across his middle proclaimed that being the only lawyer in Rocky Creek was a lucrative business. He studied a map of the town on the desk before him.

'We have a couple of spare cabins, Mr Malone. This one here is only a block back from the main street. It's very basic, just a fireplace, a bunk and a chair and table, if some previous tenant has not burned them for fuel. This one has glass in the window and, as far as I know, its roof is sound. It has a small corral behind it with a lean-to to give a bit of protection if you have any horses. Even the outhouse is in good order. Rent is eight dollars a month if you want it. The railroad prefers them to be occupied, otherwise drunks and other derelicts break into them. A few have actually been burned down. That one is not far from the livery stable and only a couple of minutes' walk to the middle of town. It's actually a prime location.'

The scout reached into his pocket and produced a ten-dollar bill. 'What if I take it for five weeks? I'm not sure how long I'll be staying.'

'That won't be a problem. I'll just write you a receipt and give you the key. If you like I can get a load of chopped firewood dropped around.'

'That's a good idea. How much extra is that?'

'Another two dollars fifty but it will last you for a week.'

'That's money well spent, Mr Lauder. I think I have it here in change.'

With his temporary home arranged, Malone went to the general store to arrange a few necessities. His camping gear was fine for out of doors but to live in a house a few more items were needed. He was leaving with his arms full of purchases when he nearly collided with a woman coming in the door. It was Nancy Crane.

'I'm sorry, Mrs Crane. I nearly trampled you there.'

It took Nancy a while to recognize Malone. Then she smiled, 'Jeff Malone . . . I didn't know you at first. You did not look quite so handsome last time I saw you. What on earth are you doing in Rocky Creek?'

'Mainly I was just travelling, but I took on a horse-breaking job for Mike Hemings at the livery stable. How's life in Rocky Creek?'

'Business has been good for Tom. The railroad is selling land that the government gave it along the right-of-way and there is all the surveying that Tom can handle.'

'And how is Julie?'

'She's fine. She was only telling me the other day that Mike Hemings is an old friend of yours.'

'That's right. We went on quite a few patrols together. He was a good soldier. It's nice to see him settled down and so happy.'

'And what about you? Have you settled down yet?'

He smiled ruefully. 'I'm not exactly in a job that lends itself to settling down. Most wives would prefer a husband who comes home every night.'

'Preferably still with his scalp,' Nancy laughed. 'But what will you do when you have killed all the Indians?'

All traces of humour went from Malone's face. 'I don't want to kill anyone . . . Indians or anyone else. I see my job as guiding the army to positions where they can enforce the government's wishes with a minimum of bloodshed. Sometimes it works, sometimes it doesn't, but I have a lot of respect for Indians. I don't pretend to know all the answers to the Indian situation and smarter men than me are still trying to figure it out, but I would hate to think of them being wiped out.'

'I'm sorry. I seem to have touched a raw nerve there. Could I make amends by inviting you to dinner tonight? I know Julie would love to see you, and Tom would be keen to hear about your latest adventures.'

Malone smiled. 'This Rocky Creek is a mighty hospitable town. For the second night in a row I am to be spared my own cooking. I would be glad to come to dinner tonight. How do I find your place?'

Nancy pointed down the road. 'See that white fence on the right? That's our front fence. Any time around six-thirty will do.'

'Can I bring anything?'

'Don't worry. Just bring yourself.'

Life seemed to be looking up for Malone and he whistled a little tune to himself as he strolled along the board-walk.

'Jeff Malone,' a voice called from behind him.

He turned to see Wilson standing behind him smiling, a large cigar jutting from the corner of his mouth. 'I thought it was you,' the gambler said. 'Don't tell me we have an Indian outbreak in Rocky Creek.'

'Not as far as I know,' Malone replied. 'I'm just picking up a bit of work until spring when the army will be out again. You look fairly prosperous; there must be some keen gamblers around here.'

'Fortunately their enthusiasm is less than their skill. I know it's a bit early in the day but would you like a drink?'

It was a bit early for Malone but he had nothing more important to do. 'Why not?'

They found a quiet table at the back of the saloon. The scout bought the drinks. Wilson had a whiskey but Malone settled for a beer. He noted that the gambler was still wearing the gun and gunbelt he had taken from Grigg.

'You're asking for trouble with that gun, Mark. A character like Grigg doesn't forget that he has sworn to kill you. You are making yourself too easy to find.'

'You worry too much, Jeff. His gang is scattered and he's on the run. I wouldn't worry too much about him.'

'Don't be too sure. Grigg is very good at what he does. That's why he's lasted so long. He'd give his eye teeth to know that the two of us are in the one place like this.'

141

'He might steer clear of it, too. I read where you shot it out with Clem Ryan. He was supposed to be hell on wheels with a gun. I don't know if Grigg is as good. I doubt he'd be keen to take you on in a gunfight.'

'Grigg is smarter than that. He won't take any risks he don't have to. He might use a rifle from long range or a shotgun from a dark alley. I really believe that he will come after us when it suits him. He's not interested in a reputation as a fair fighter. The meaner his reputation the better he likes it. His aim is to keep people scared.'

'He's not scaring me,' Wilson said defiantly.

'I wish I could say the same.'

'Do you know that the Cranes live here?'

'Yes. I met Nancy just a while ago. She asked me round to dinner tonight.'

'They have never asked me to dinner and I probably saw more of them than you did.' A note of jealousy had crept into the gambler's voice. 'I suppose they

142

disapprove of my profession.'

'Maybe they do. I doubt that Indian scouts rate any higher than you with some folks though.' Malone finished his beer and stood up. 'I have to go now and fix up the cabin I'm renting. I'll see you around Mark.'

'I owe you a drink, Jeff.'

'Don't worry, I won't let you forget that.'

★ ★ ★

Zack Gilmore opened the telegram that had just been delivered to his office. He looked small behind his massive desk but his weathered face lost its usual woebegone expression as he read the message. He knew that Grigg would pay handsomely for the information he held. 'Fred,' he called to his clerk, 'come in here with your notepad.'

A nervous young man hurried into the office. Gilmore, despite his lack of size, was a bully who enjoyed keeping his staff in a constant state of apprehension. 'Note this, Fred, and it will be your job if you don't get it right.' He threw the telegraph across the desk. 'Thank the sender of this message by telegraph and wire through ten dollars with it. Take the money out of petty cash. Now send another telegraph to Mr Harold Foster care of Murray's Hotel, Thomasville, Nebraska. It is to say 'Clients one and two located. Contact me. Gilmore'. Now get that away as quick as you can and let me know when it has been sent.'

★   ★   ★

Malone felt strangely awkward as he knocked on the Cranes' door that night. The house was so neat with its fresh paint and curtained windows that he felt out of place. This was not the world he knew. His nerve was starting to fail him when the door opened.

Julie looked a vision, more beautiful than he had remembered and all his doubts disappeared when she smiled.

'Jeff, come in. It's good to see you. How are you?'

She placed a small, soft hand in Malone's. He wanted to hold it forever but then remembered himself and dropped it as though it was red hot. Awkwardly he followed her into a small sitting-room where Nancy and Tom Crane were waiting. They greeted him warmly and showed him to a comfortable chair while Nancy took his hat. Only as he passed it to her did the scout suddenly realize how sweat-stained and battered it was.

Tom opened the conversation asking about the encounter with Grigg's gang at the trading post.

Malone gave a shortened version of what had happened and asked how they were enjoying their new home. All agreed that the town was a good one and the future looked promising.

'I hear you are breaking in a couple of horses for Mike Hemings,' Julie said. 'I love horses. I have a nice pony that I keep at Mike's stables. His name is Jeb.'

'I know,' Malone told her. 'I've seen him. He looks a very good pony.'

'Do you still have that nice horse you were riding when we met you?' Nancy asked.

'Yes. I hope to have Major for years yet. He's the best horse I ever had. He'll be hard to replace.'

'I'd like to see you breaking horses,' said Julie.

'Come around tomorrow about nine. I'll be starting on them then, but there won't be a lot to see. I believe in taking them quietly.'

'What, no rearing and bucking? I thought all western horses were broken that way.'

'Horses off the open range often put up a fight because they are used to running wild, but these two have had a bit of experience with people and are not as frightened.'

'So they won't buck?' Julie sounded disappointed.

'They might. Bucking can be in-herited and the odd horse will buck no

146

matter how carefully you take it. You are never quite sure what a young horse will do when it's first mounted.'

'What do you do if it bucks?' Tom asked. 'I've heard some bronc busters go for them with the whip and spurs and teach it that bucking is no use.'

'I just sit there as quietly as I can. Most young horses are only bucking out of fear and I can't see the point in hurting them and frightening them more. I let them learn that there is nothing to be feared from me. That way they get over their fright and usually don't buck again.'

'From what I've heard that would seem to be a novel approach here in the West,' Julie told him.

'Not really. The bronc busters who fight every horse, soon find some that can fight better than them. They get busted up and most lose their nerve. At the finish they spoil every horse they touch. There are plenty of others who take horses quietly and they are the ones that stay in the game longest. They are also the ones that most ranchers are happy to give their work to.'

The meal was superb and by then Malone was completely relaxed. Julie had a good sense of humour and the conversation and laughs flowed easily. It had been a long time since the scout had enjoyed himself so much.

After dinner Nancy and Tom washed the dishes while Julie took Malone back to the sitting-room. 'Tom said you are welcome to try some of his cigars, Jeff, if you would like to smoke.'

'Thanks, Julie but I don't smoke. Indians can smell tobacco smoke a long way off. In my line of work it is not a good idea.'

'You must have some minor vices.'

'No minor ones,' he joked.

The evening passed pleasantly and Malone was loath to go but feared that he might wear out his welcome. Reluctantly he took his leave after thanking his hosts.

Frank Rydell just happened to be going home on the opposite side of the road when he saw Malone leaving the Cranes'. He was much relieved as he feared that the scout might have moved on. With friends in town, he was much more likely to stay until Grigg arrived. He did not know when that would be but knew that the outlaw would move quickly.

11

Next morning Malone started on the two horses. He had the buckskin in the small round corral when Julie arrived. The horse was the more nervous of the two so he started on it first. Malone was holding it by a halter and was rubbing it down with an old saddle blanket. Gradually the horse lost its high-headed nervous stance and began to relax. He dragged the blanket over the animal's tail, then over its head and flapped it around its legs without the animal showing any fear.

'How is the work going?' Julie asked.

'It's pretty easy so far. This horse was already half broken. He's smart, too, and is learning well.'

'He looks as though he'll be a nice horse.'

'I think he will. Would you like to come in here and say howdy to him?'

'If you're sure I won't frighten him.'

'There's less chance of him taking fright now than there will be later if he sees a woman in a skirt. While so many new things are happening he accepts strange sights a lot better.'

'Are you saying that I'm a strange sight, Jeff?'

'Er . . . no . . . I mean he's not used to seeing ladies. I've seen range-raised horses that really came unglued the first time they saw a lady in a skirt. Just come in here quietly where he can see you and walk up beside me. Don't make any sudden moves.'

The buckskin snorted and threw up its head but allowed Julie to approach until she stood beside Malone.

The scout stroked the animal's head for a minute or so until he was sure that it was relaxed and said, 'Just put your hand out and let him sniff it. Hold it still, he won't bite you.'

Cautiously the horse stretched out its neck and sniffed the outstretched hand. It brushed the fingers briefly with its nose and stood back.

'He trusts you now,' Malone said. 'A horse won't put its nose on anything that it is frightened of. Now, without moving suddenly, put your hand out and gently touch him on the nose. Then just rub the side of his jaw.'

'His nose feels like velvet,' Julie said, as she stroked the animal. 'He seems nice and friendly.'

'He probably is, but be careful, he can still get a sudden fright. Stand well up at his shoulder. He can cow-kick a long way forward and some horses kick before they think.'

For the next hour Malone and Julie worked around the horse, picking up its feet, leading it and generally making it accustomed to people. They were enjoying themselves, but the scout did not want the horse to become stale. 'That's all for this fellow today. Young horses get bored easily so it's best to keep training periods short. I'll let this one go and bring in the chestnut one now.'

They repeated the process with the chestnut horse. It seemed even more responsive than the buckskin had been and Julie enjoyed herself immensely. Her clothes were dusty and her hair dishevelled by the time they finished for the day, but she was laughing and happy.

'I'll put a saddle on them tomorrow and see how they take it,' Malone said as he walked her home.

'I'll make sure that I'm there to watch,' Julie said.

* ★ ★

Jonas Grigg bore little resemblance to a wanted bandit. Clean-shaven and neatly dressed in town clothes and a derby hat he was the picture of respectability. In keeping with his new image he no longer wore a gun openly although he had a short-barrelled .44 in a shoulder holster. He read the telegram again and could scarcely believe his luck, Malone and Wilson both in the same town. In his new guise he looked a little out of place talking across a saloon table to a character like Ike Elkins.

Ike was a small, scrawny weasel of a man who was much tougher than he looked. He wore a pair of old-fashioned Navy Colts and was not afraid to use them. It was a brave man who knowingly crossed the little pistolero because he had a violent temper, was absolutely ruthless and feared no one. He said softly, 'You reckon both the *hombres* you're after are in the same town, Jonas? That's a piece of luck.'

'You're right there, Ike. The two of them are in a little town in Wyoming called Rocky Creek. Do you know of it?'

'I seem to have heard of it but have never been there.'

'It's only a couple of days' ride west of here on a branch line of the Union Pacific. How soon can you get a couple of men together?'

'How many guns do you need to kill two men?'

'Those two are only part of the deal. I thought that since I had to go all that way, I might rob the bank while I'm in the area. We could break away to the south-west towards Salt Lake City. I've never been there and no one will look for me there among the Mormons.'

'I reckon that as well as ourselves we need at least three good men or maybe even four. We don't know how strong the law is around there.'

'Make it four, Ike, just to be on the safe side.'

'Joe Meithke is keen to join us. Do we ask him, Jonas?'

'No. Meithke is mad. He'll only draw attention to us. Take only men you know to be smart and who will follow orders.'

'Marty Reece might be a good recruit. To date he's only been stealing cattle and horses, but I think he might be handy to us. He's smart and knows his way about. I don't know what he's like with a gun, though.'

'We don't need too many top gun

hands. They're inclined to shoot instead of running. There's no need to shoot up a town if you get in and out of the bank fast.'

'What about horses?'

'Get good ones and grain feed them. They're getting their winter coats now so don't groom them too much. It's better if they look a bit rough. Get horses that are not likely to be identified as being stolen. We don't want some sheriff stopping us on the way because of stolen horses.'

'How much time do we have?'

'I'll give you a week to get horses and men and four days to get to Rocky Creek. We might need to hide out for a couple of days and spy out the lie of the land before we hit the bank.'

'Can you do it in that time?'

'I reckon so, Abe Conlon and Jud Haskins are not so far from here as we speak. This place is a mite hot for them and I reckon they'll be keen to work elsewhere. Conlon's a good man. We can use him and if Haskins wasn't good, Abe wouldn't team up with him. They'll do if you can get them. Tell them we'll go equal shares once I recoup the expenses for setting things up.'

* * *

The next day, Malone took the buckskin horse into the small corral. Julie was there again. She was fond of horses and was enjoying working with the young ones.

The scout put a hackamore on the buckskin and led him to the rail where he had left his saddle. While holding the reins, he slapped a saddle blanket around the horse again. This was familiar to the horse and he stood calmly. Then Malone heaved up the saddle and settled it gently on the horse's back. The animal jammed down its tail and shuffled nervously but offered no resistance. Very carefully the scout reached under for the cinch, quickly ran the latigo through it and hitched it to the rigging on the near side. The horse humped its back a little as he caught up the flank cinch and also fastened that.

'Is it ready to mount now?' Julie asked.

'No, I have to ease the cinches up gradually. I don't want him bucking yet.'

When he had the cinches to his satisfaction, Malone hooked the reins over the saddle horn and let the horse free. The animal looked over its shoulder, saw the saddle and jumped in alarm. A loose stirrup rattled and the horse dropped its head and crow-hopped across the corral. After a couple of futile attempts to throw the saddle, it trotted a few circuits of the corral and allowed Malone to catch it.

'I think that one will give you some trouble,' Julie ventured.

'He might not. He was objecting to the cinch, not the weight of the saddle.' As he said that Malone took the cheekstrap of the hackamore in his left hand, pulled the horse's head toward him and stepped smoothly into the saddle. The rider immediately picked up his off-side stirrup, and evened his reins. A gentle squeeze of the calves and the horse took a tentative step and stopped. 'You're allowed to walk,' Malone told the animal quietly.

For maybe a second the horse stood there, then urged by another gentle squeeze it stepped out again. Weaving like a drunken sailor it made its first circuit of the corral. Then it seemed to realize what was wanted and began to step out freely. Malone started turning it then on either side, releasing rein pressure as soon as the horse obeyed the cue. Finally he stopped it and backed the animal a couple of steps. Then he dismounted and remounted a couple of times before declaring, 'That's enough for a first ride. You went well, little horse.'

'Is that all you are doing with this one today?' Julie seemed surprised.

'That's plenty for a first ride, now

we'll have a try at the chestnut.'

The chestnut horse showed little interest in proceedings as Malone cinched the saddle on its back. It laid back its ears and trotted around the corral when turned loose but made no attempt to buck.

'It looks like you will have an easy time with this one,' Julie said.

Malone was not so sure. 'This one is too quiet. It's the ones like this that often wake up with a fright. It's more natural for them to object a bit.'

He reined up the horse and very carefully mounted. For a moment it stood, then snorted and hurled itself into a flying rear. When it hit the ground stiff-legged, the chestnut threw itself back under the rider with a reverse buck that slammed him against the pommel of the saddle. Then it spun to the side dropping its near-side shoulder leaving Malone struggling to retain the stirrup on that side. But the sheer intensity of the effort sapped the animal's strength quickly and in seconds it reverted to a series of feeble kicks as it galloped around the corral.

Malone sat quietly and the horse was happy to stop when he checked it with the hackamore. A gentle squeeze evoked another half-hearted buck but finding that a waste of energy, the horse tentatively took a step forward. 'Good boy,' the rider said and rubbed the side of its neck.

Gradually the horse gained confidence and started walking around the corral with no more objection to being ridden.

When Malone dismounted and unsaddled the animal, Julie asked, 'Are they both broken now?'

'The work is only just starting. Now I have to teach them their paces and how to stop and turn and do all the things good horses need to do. Getting them to accept a rider is only one of the early lessons. I'm glad this one stopped when it did. He took a bit of riding.'

'Will he always buck?'

'Chances are he won't as long as

nobody gets too careless and gives him an easy victory over a rider. The horse that throws a rider will always try again. He might wait weeks or months, but he will try again. When these are safe to take out of the corral would you like to come riding with me? They settle easier if they have a sensible horse with them. You and Jeb would be mighty handy.'

'I'd love it,' Julie said. 'It looks like an interesting time coming up.'

12

Ike Elkins was the first of the gang to reach Rocky Creek. They were travelling in ones and twos and approaching from different directions so they would not attract attention. After brief stops to familiarize themselves with the town they would assemble at a disused line cabin a few miles out of town that Rydell had organized for them. With money sent by the outlaw, he had hired a wagon from Hemings and stocked the cabin with food for the gang and fodder for their horses. He had also repaired it to the point where it was rough but habitable.

The little gunman wandered into the Gilded Lily and saw Wilson engrossed in a poker game at the back of the saloon. He had not met the gambler but recognized him by the description he had been given. As he sipped his whiskey alone at the bar, he knew that Wilson's days were numbered. Following Grigg's orders he resolved to attract no attention and was finishing his drink when things suddenly went wrong.

Matt Harper had been the town's sheriff in the few years it had existed. It had once been a wild railroad camp and he had been kept busy. But now the track layers were gone and things were much quieter. Gradually reflexes honed by danger relaxed as the sheriff found his job getting easier. It had been months since he had needed to draw one of the two big Army Colts that he wore and it was more than a year since he had fired a shot in anger.

Years before he had arrested Ike Elkins in another town for being drunk and disorderly. That was before Elkins had attained wanted outlaw status. The sheriff was doing his daily round of the town when he saw something familiar about the lone drinker at the bar. Trying to remember where he had seen the man, but still unsuspecting, Harper walked closer.

Elkins saw the lawman and recognized him instantly. Thinking that he was about to be arrested, the little man went into action. A revolver was already coming clear of its holster as the outlaw turned with the speed of a striking snake.

Harper's hands flew to his guns, but surprise and easy living had dulled his reflexes. His weapons were just clearing leather as Elkins started shooting.

The first shot took the sheriff in the upper chest and he staggered under the impact. Another hit him on the hip knocking him to the ground and Elkins' third bullet hit the lawman's arm as he tried to raise his gun.

The outlaw ran past his victim as he struggled on the floor and collided with a passer-by as he burst from the saloon. A vicious swipe with a gun barrel dropped the man to the boardwalk and hardly slowed the gunman's flight. He reached his horse and flung himself into the saddle. Raking the animal with his spurs, he galloped away.

Malone heard the shots and the galloping horse, but was riding the buckskin in the corral and could not see what was happening. 'Sounds like trouble,' he told Julie, who was watching from outside the corral.

Seconds later, Hemings came out from the stables. 'There's been a shooting at the saloon,' he said. 'Someone filled Matt Harper with lead.'

'Is he dead?'

'Not yet, but he's been hit a few times. Nobody's sure how badly yet. We're getting a bit of a posse together. Will you join us? Your tracking skill would be a big help.'

'I'll be with you as quick as I can. Who are we looking for?'

'Nobody knows who he is, some little guy in a brown coat riding a bay horse. That's the only description of him. But we know that he's very fast with a gun and doesn't miss too many shots.'

'Poor Sheriff Harper,' Julie said. 'I'd best leave you two to start organizing your posse. Be careful.'

'We will,' Malone promised, as he began unsaddling the horse.

Fifteen minutes later, Malone met the posse, seven citizens including Hemings. Some were unlikely to strike terror into the hearts of evil-doers as they were middle-aged and indifferently mounted, but they would be useful if the pursuit was not too drawn out. The posse had trampled the tracks around the hitching rail and the scout had to ride a fair distance before he picked up the hoofprints he wanted. They were deep and wide apart indicating that they were made by a galloping horse.

Apart from being freshly shod, the horse's tracks were not unique. No special shoes or unusual leg action were reflected in the prints. Malone knew that the horse would be hard to follow once it got to well-used roads.

'Keep about fifty yards behind me so I can get a bit of time to look at tracks,' Malone told the others. Then he touched Major lightly with his heels and loosened the reins. The bay horse broke into an easy rocking-chair canter. When the scout was the required distance ahead, Hemings led off the rest of the posse at a smart trot.

Elkins made no attempt to disguise his tracks until his mount started to tire. He had a good horse but was realistic enough to assume that some posse members would also be riding good animals. It was time to be cunning for he had no intention of leading the hunters to the line cabin. He would lose them before circling back.

Removing the lariat from his saddle, the outlaw flipped a loop over a bush beside the trail, dallied the rope around the horn and dragged the bush from the ground. By dragging it in his wake he used the bush like a broom to wipe out his tracks. It bounced about and did not strike every print but it made tracking a bit more difficult and when leaving the trail for sage-covered areas the bush concealed the prints really well.

Malone received the first hint when he noticed that the hoof prints were disappearing. He could see the drag marks of the bush and read his quarry's intentions. He's smart but will need to know more tricks than that, the scout told himself. The Indian trackers who taught him would not have been so easily fooled. They would follow the leaves that broke from the bush as it was dragged along. They did not look for strange things but rather natural things in unnatural places, like stones turned over or leaves from a certain bush in places where there were no similar types.

Elkins was no fool and when he thought he had slowed the hunters, he turned off the trail and rode into the sage-covered low hills through which the trail wound. His horse was tiring, but he reasoned that the posse would also be pushing their mounts hard to try to close the gap between them. A short distance off the trail, he abandoned the tattered bush and rode east for another few minutes. This time he deliberately rode across a patch of bare red earth where the eastward-pointing hoofprints showed clearly. Then, riding into the sage, he turned in a wide loop and rode west crossing the road again about half a mile further than where he had left it. He dismounted long enough to brush out the tracks on the road carefully with a small piece of bush and then rode for the hideout.

The weather was getting worse. The skies darkened, the north wind blew strongly and sleet began to fall. Snow was not far away. Some of the posse members started looking anxious.

When he saw the hoofprints showing so plainly on the bare red earth Malone knew that it was a trick. A man as careful as this one had been would not suddenly become careless.

'We're going the wrong way,' the scout told the posse.

'But his tracks still point that way,' one man argued.

'He wants us to think he went that

way; I'm going to look in the opposite direction.'

'You won't have much time,' Hemings told him. 'There's a blizzard on the way. I think we should head for home.'

'I'm damn sure we should,' another posse member added. Already he was wishing that he had not come. 'If that killer is out in this he'll freeze to death anyway.'

Malone hated to admit it but he knew that the others were right. 'I think we will have to turn around. But before I go I want to get some idea of where to look for that character later. The way he's hiding his tracks looks to me that he doesn't intend to run far. I think he has a hideout around here somewhere. You turn back, I'll have one more look around and catch up with you.'

When the others left, Malone rode in a wide circle. The wind was moving the sage about and by the time he had crossed the trail he had found nothing. He was sure though that the gunman had gone in that direction. The first few flakes of snow were falling when he found what he sought. They were there on a bare piece of ground, hoof prints pointing to the badlands in the west. The rider had abandoned all cunning and was riding fast and straight. He was somewhere west of the road.

At the rate the snow was falling, any tracks would soon be covered so Malone could only commit the place to his memory and ride back to Rocky Creek. He was sure in his own mind that the mystery gunman was hiding somewhere in the area rather than trying simply to outrun the law. Was he seeking some temporary refuge from the posse and the weather, or did he have some reason for staying in the vicinity of Rocky Creek?

Arriving back in town, he took Major to Hemings' livery stable as it provided better shelter than the lean-to behind his own cabin. He asked his friend if he had any news of the sheriff.

'He's not as bad as I thought,' Hemings said. 'His arm is broken but the bullets didn't penetrate so well through his heavy winter clothes. If no infection sets in the doctor seems to think he'll recover fully.'

'He was lucky. One of the possemen told me that the gunman used a Navy Colt. They're very accurate guns but the .36 bullet doesn't have the power of the .44. That's the only failing of the Navy. If they miss a vital spot, they often only wound. The sheriff can thank his lucky stars.'

'Did you find anything after we left?'

'I picked up his tracks but the snow beat me. He had crossed to the western side of the trail. The country over there's mighty rough, but I reckon he knew something about the place that I didn't. Are there any ranches or cabins out there that you know of?'

Hemings shook his head. 'I'm not very familiar with that area, but as far as I know, nobody lives there. When I see Pete Manson I'll ask him. Pete used to work on ranches in this area, but the railroad was given a lot of the open range by the government as payment for their tracks. The Cheyenne also wiped out a couple of ranches that were here before the town. I don't get out of town much and have only been here for two years so am not really familiar with what's outside of town. If anyone knows what's out there it will be Pete. But do you think it's worthwhile to keep looking for this man? When we were riding back, the general opinion was that the mystery gunman was just running in panic and would probably freeze to death anyway.'

'I've seen enough of those characters to know that they don't panic. I think our man knew exactly what he was doing.'

13

The blizzard blew for three days, snow piled up in deep drifts and nobody ventured abroad. Freezing to death, pneumonia, or at least, frostbite were real possibilities.

Malone spent most of the time in his cabin sitting near the fire and wondering about the gunman they had chased. Matt Harper remembered his identity. It was Ike Elkins, a small-time crook when first they had met but later he had graduated to robbing banks. According to the wounded sheriff's recollections, Elkins never acted alone. The scout thought about that a lot. Was the gunman just passing through, or had he planned some crime in the area? With whom would he be working?

Hemings was huddled over a small Sibley stove at the back of the stables when Malone arrived to check on his horse. They spoke for a while before the conversation came around to Elkins.

'I have a feeling that he's hanging about here somewhere,' Malone declared.

Hemings was not so sure. 'If he is, I think it's only because of the weather and I reckon there's every chance him and his horse are out there somewhere frozen.'

'Did you get a chance to talk to that old cowhand?'

'No, I reckon the weather's keeping him close to home. I'll let you know what I find out when I catch up with him. That outlaw has really got under your skin, hasn't he?'

'He sure has. He made me look like an idiot the other day. I want to square accounts with him, but I also feel that there's something in the wind. Sheriff Harper reckoned that he never acts alone. I wonder who his friends are and where they are right now?'

'Nobody else thought you were an idiot. We all thought that no one else could have done better. He had us fooled into thinking he was going east instead of west. Forget about him, Jeff. He's either dead, or a long way away by now.'

Malone shook his head. 'You're probably right, Mike, but I have a funny feeling about that *hombre*. This weather has been a mixed blessing though. I know that Jonas Grigg won't be here until the weather improves, so for a while I can stop looking over my shoulder.'

'I didn't think you were worried about Grigg.'

'That's an act I put on in public, but privately I must admit to the odd sleepless night. If his intelligence service is half as good as it's reputed to be, he already knows that two people he has sworn to kill are in the same place at the same time. I doubt that Grigg will be able to resist those circumstances. When the weather breaks, I reckon he'll be on his way here.'

His friend disagreed. 'I think Grigg has more important matters on his mind. His gang's broken up and the law is probably hot on his heels. If I was him I'd be riding hard for Mexico.'

The blizzard eventually stopped and later that day Hemings came out to where Malone was riding the newly broken horses in the corral. They had settled down and were responding to his cues.

'Jeff,' the livery-man called. 'I've just been talking to Pete Manson. He seems to remember that one of the old ranches had a line cabin out in the area where that gunman shook us off. It was built to stop cattle drifting into the badlands. He never worked there but reckons it might still be standing.'

'Did he give any directions?'

'He has never been there, but thinks it was at the headwaters of Duncan's Creek.'

'Where's that?'

'Remember that creek that ran across the trail about ten miles out of town where we chased that gunman? It runs back into some mighty rough country but that's where the shack will be, somewhere along that creek.'

'I might take a ride out there when I'm sure that the weather has settled down a bit,' Malone said.

* * *

Marty Reece and Grigg travelled together. They came up the trail from the south and had no trouble finding the old cabin. Elkins had given very good directions. Jud Haskins was already there.

Abe Conlon was riding alone. His job was to check the situation in the town and study the bank's routine. Conlon knew nobody and had never been to Rocky Creek so his chances of being recognized as a bandit were slim. He had been told to find Rydell in town and to check on the whereabouts of Malone and Wilson while gathering information about the bank. Conlon was a good planner and Grigg trusted his judgement.

Elkins met his companions as they dismounted at the cabin door. He had a rifle clutched in his hands.

'You look nervous, Ike,' Grigg chuckled. 'Did you think we were the law?'

'I thought you might have been. The sheriff in Rocky Creek tried to arrest me. I shot him and took off. I thought there would probably be a posse after me.'

All good humour went from Grigg's voice. 'I hope you didn't leave a clear trail to here.'

'I'm not that dumb, Jonas. I set a false trail to take them the other way if they were trying to run my tracks. A blizzard hit that day so I'm not sure anyone even came after me.'

'Abe Conlon's coming through Rocky Creek,' Reece reminded the others. 'He'll let us know if any posse is hunting Ike.'

'Lou Williams is coming up from the south. He wouldn't appreciate running into a posse,' the outlaw leader growled.

Elkins allowed himself a little laugh.

'A posse would not appreciate running into him either.'

'I don't want anyone running into posses. We can't afford to lose anyone at all,' Grigg reminded him. 'Now, let's get our horses put away and get in out of the cold.'

★   ★   ★

Abe Conlon hitched his horse to the rail outside the saloon and headed into the Gilded Lily where he hoped to find Rydell. He was a tall, commanding figure of a man who still retained the bearing of the military officer he once had been. But being on the losing side in the Civil War was only the start of his troubles; a hot temper and a fast gun had combined to start his journey on the outlaw trail. He walked with a slight limp from an old leg wound and was dressed in good quality clothes. Even if they could not see the big pair of guns concealed by his overcoat, he was a man people noticed. 'I'm looking for

Frank Rydell,' he told the bartender.

'That's him at that table near the door, the one drinking alone.'

Conlon ordered a bottle and crossed the room to where Rydell sat staring at a half-empty glass. The latter looked up in alarm at the tall man who joined him at the table.

'I believe we have a mutual friend,' he said, as he sat down.

'Have we?' Rydell had downed more than his fair share of whiskey that night and was slow to comprehend.

'I think you know who I mean. You sent him a telegraph recently.'

Recognition dawned.

'Er . . . that's right. What can I do for you?'

'I was hoping that you could give me a few details about a couple of matters in this town.'

'Sure I can. You're probably lookin' for Wilson and Malone. See that gambler over there in the corner? That's Wilson. He's wearing Jonas Grigg's gun. I hear that Grigg has offered a reward for the return of that gun. Is that right?'

'I believe it is, but don't do anything yet. There are more important matters at stake. Tell me about the bank.'

'It's on the main street. There are bars on the back windows but none on the front.'

'How many doors?'

'One front and one back. Front doors are double.'

'How many work there?'

'A manager and two clerks.'

'When is the most money deposited?'

'The local businesses all seem to bank Monday mornings.'

'How often does the bank send money to its head office?'

'I'm not sure, but it's probably on the Wednesday coach.'

'What about the law?'

'The sheriff's laid up at present. A gunman passing through town shot him full of holes. A few local citizens formed a posse but they got nowhere. That army scout, Malone, is in town too, but he ain't here tonight. He shot Clem Ryan, but the story is that he had a lot of luck. He could be the only one Grigg needs to watch. Hemings, from the livery stable, is ex-cavalry, but he's certainly no gunfighter.'

'What about Wilson, the gambler?'

'He's a damn fool, is all. He won't get caught up in law business. From what I hear that friend of ours intends to finish both Malone and Wilson. I've heard he'll pay anyone who fixes one or both of that pair for good.'

'Could be.' Conlon allowed a slight smile to cross his features. He had little time for men like Rydell but they came in useful occasionally. 'You did well, Rydell. I'm sure our mutual friend will be suitably grateful. Now I'm going for a walk around the town, have a good meal and move on.'

Malone was getting the two horses used to being around town and regularly rode them along the street. They soon stopped spooking at reflections in shop windows and people who emerged unexpectedly from doorways. He was steering the buckskin pony through a muddy patch in the road when he noticed Conlon's horse at the hitching rail. It was a big iron grey, well built and in perfect condition for hard work. He had not seen the animal around and surmised that a stranger was in town. As he drew level with the horse, a tall stranger emerged from the saloon and took the grey's reins. He saw Malone looking at the animal.

'Howdy,' the scout said. 'Nice horse.'

'Not bad,' Conlon replied. His tone of voice discouraged further conversation.

As he rode on, something about the tall stranger told Malone that this man was no ordinary cattleman. His clothes were too clean and the quality of both horse and saddlery indicated a man of considerable means. The wary way that the stranger looked about was the action of one who did not normally live among friends.

14

Wilson laid down his cards and pushed back his chair. The night had been reasonably rewarding for him and he had finished a few dollars to the good. 'That's it for the night, gentlemen. I'm going now for a well-earned night's rest. Thank you for your contribution to my board and lodgings.'

'I'll get my money back tomorrow night,' a big freighter threatened.

'I doubt that your luck will change in a few hours. It seems to be running strongly against us at present,' another card player said ruefully.

'You'll find me here again tomorrow, gentlemen, if you think your luck is running stronger your way. Good evening.'

Wilson walked out of the saloon, paused to light a cigar and started strolling home along the boardwalk in front of the shops. Most of Rocky Creek's citizens had retired for the night so he found nothing unusual in being the only person on the street. He was quietly satisfied with the way the cards had fallen to him and the drink he had allowed himself before leaving had put him in a carefree mood. He had never really taken Jonas Grigg's threat seriously and the outlaw was far from his mind as he walked.

That was until he passed the mouth of a dark alley and the double click of a gun being cocked brought back the threat with terrifying reality. His relaxed mood vanished in a split second.

'Don't move,' a muffled voice ordered.

Wilson froze. His life hung in the balance and he knew it.

'Get your hands up and step in here.'

'Don't shoot. You can have my wallet; I won't give you any trouble.'

'Dang sure you won't. Unbuckle that gunbelt and pass it over here. Be very careful how you do it.'

All his life Wilson had played the

odds. He knew that the man in the alley was not Grigg. He was also aware that in the poor light the gunman might not see him draw his gun and that shots fired in such circumstances often missed.

Wilson gambled again.

Carefully he unbuckled the gunbelt but as he passed it over he snatched the big Smith & Wesson from its holster. The gunman heard him cock the hammer and immediately fired. Wilson's luck had deserted him. The bullet took the gambler on the chest and punched him backwards against the wall of a building. As a reflex action, he jerked the trigger and his own shot went wild. Cursing in fear and anger the gunman fired two more shots as the gambler fell. One hit him in the side of the head and the other missed.

The gunman snatched up the fallen gunbelt, wasted precious seconds feeling on the ground for the revolver and finally finding it just as he heard boots on the boardwalk. The saloon patrons had surely heard the shots and were coming to investigate.

Streaks of red flame and the roar of a gun from the alley checked the advance of even the most curious. They jumped back into doorways unsure of how many guns were out there and exactly where they were.

The gunman ran back down the alley to a horse he had tied behind the buildings. He looped the gunbelt over the saddle horn and hauled himself aboard his mount. The sound of boots on the boardwalk told him that the pursuers' fright had worn off. He drove home the spurs and fled.

The men emerging cautiously to investigate heard the pounding hoofs and knew that the shooter was escaping. With drawn guns they abandoned all caution and sprinted to the alley and there they found the body of Wilson.

Next morning Matt Harper sent a messenger for Malone. The sheriff was still recuperating from his wounds and had given up trying to uphold the law from his bed. His wife showed the scout through to where the injured lawman lay.

'Excuse me for not getting up, Malone, and for not shaking hands, but it is a bit awkward with a broken right arm. You're probably wondering why I sent for you.'

'I guess it's something to do with last night's murder. The whole town's talking about it.'

'That's part of it,' Harper admitted. 'How would you like a deputy's job until I'm on my feet again? I've talked it over with the town committee and I can offer sixty dollars a month plus a feed allowance for your horses. Are you interested?'

'Could be, but come spring I'll be back with the army. Is there any special reason why you picked me?'

'I heard good reports from the members of that posse you took out the other day and you have a good reputation with a gun.'

'I have had my share of luck, but

I'm no *pistolero.*'

'That's the last thing I want. Until recently things have been quiet around here. I want someone who can keep it that way.'

'Not all folks would agree that I would make a good lawman. I've heard it said that I did wrong by striking a deal with Grigg and then letting him go.'

Harper waved his good arm dismissively. 'Take no notice of them. You saved the strongbox and probably the lives of some people on the coach. In my book, saving innocent lives is more important than shooting outlaws. All I need is for you to keep the lid on this town for a couple of weeks till I am right again.'

'I think that might be a pretty tall order. There was a murder last night and it may be that Jonas Grigg was behind it. He had sworn to kill Wilson and to get back his gun that Wilson had. The killer left Wilson's wallet and only took the gunbelt and gun. A couple of gunmen have passed through here recently. One of them shot you and the one I saw yesterday was the same breed. Grigg could be gathering another gang around him. He has plenty to interest him here in Rocky Creek.'

'Why is that?'

'From a business point of view you have a bank here that looks like it could be opened with a hair pin and, from a personal point of view, there is me. Grigg has sworn to kill me. He seems to have got Wilson, so I am next on his list. If I'm here acting as the law, the temptation could be too much. He might hit this town and try to fix the bank and me at the same time. So making me a deputy might not keep this place a peaceful town. Are you sure you don't want to reconsider your offer?'

'Would you prefer to run?'

'No. Here is as good as any place to take him on, but I don't want to bring trouble on the town.'

'I think you are worrying too much about what Grigg *might* do rather than what he has the resources *to* do. I'm willing to take a chance on being wrong. Keep the lid on the town for a month or so and worry about Grigg if he comes. Will you take the job?'

'I'll give it a try.'

'Good. I'll swear you in and give you the keys to the sheriff's office.'

* * *

Rydell was smart enough not to ride direct to the cabin where the gang was assembling. There was no pursuit, but he was taking no chances. Only when he was sure that he had covered his tracks, did he ride for the hide-out.

He arrived there just after daybreak. The outlaws were already having breakfast. They ate early before travellers were about and then dowsed the cooking fires until after nightfall. Marty Reece was acting as a sentry. He saw Rydell approaching and, as he knew him, he allowed the rider through to the shack.

Rydell dismounted at the cabin door and took the gunbelt from where it hung on his saddlehorn. Holding his trophy he entered the cabin. The rest of the gang were seated around an improvised table on wooden blocks that served as chairs.

'Got a present for you, Jonas,' Rydell announced cheerfully.

Grigg looked up and his face froze. 'Is that what I think it is?'

'Sure is. I heard you wanted it back pretty bad so I got it for you last night.'

'How did you get it last night?' Grigg's voice dropped almost to a whisper. His eyes became narrow slits.

'I shot that gambler Wilson, last night in Rocky Creek. No one saw me and I got clean away . . . I covered my tracks comin' here.' Rydell suddenly realized that Grigg was not as happy as he had expected him to be.

Grigg stood up his face livid with anger. 'You fool. The last thing I needed was to have the town stirred up.'

'Hell, Jonas, I thought — '

'That's the whole trouble, you jackass, you *didn't* think. Give me that gun.'

Nervously, Rydell passed over the weapon. All hopes of a reward from Grigg had vanished in the face of the outlaw's blazing rage.

Grigg snatched the gun, broke it and checked that it was loaded. Angrily he snapped it shut again.

'You won't find anything wrong with it, Jonas . . . it works fine.' Rydell tried desperately to appease the outlaw's anger.

'Good.'

With one smooth movement, Grigg cocked and fired the weapon straight into the other man's chest. Rydell crashed to the floor under the impact of the heavy bullet. Momentarily, his eyes stared in disbelief and then the life went from them.

Those inside the cabin looked on in amazement as the noise and the cloud of gunsmoke seemed to fill the room.

'Was that really necessary, Jonas?' Conlon asked mildly.

'It was. Do you want to argue?'

'Now doesn't seem a good time. Rydell was a greedy fool and certainly some sort of a reprimand was due, but that did strike me as being rather extreme.'

'He won't cause me any more trouble,' Grigg announced. 'Now let's plant him somewhere out in the brush. We don't want anyone finding him too soon.'

'What about his horse?' Elkins asked.

'It ain't worth much,' the leader told him. 'Pull the saddle and bridle off it and let it go. We got better horses and don't need that crowbait. Anyone wants anything from Rydell can have it, but I don't think he had anything worth taking.'

'Jonas,' said Williams, who had not risen from the table, 'I wish you wouldn't shoot people at mealtimes.

That *hombre* damn near fell in my breakfast.'

'If he did you would have started eatin' him,' Haskins joked.

*　*　*

Malone, the Cranes and a few others attended the gambler's funeral, and after that he made enquiries around the town. His first thought was that the gunman he had seen previously had returned, but one glance at where the shooter's horse had been tethered changed his mind. The tracks were those of a barefoot horse with broken and chipped feet. No professional gunman would trust his life to such a mount and the stranger's iron grey had been well shod. The killer was probably a local man because many horses only used for short rides around town were left unshod as were many cow ponies.

When he started asking around town about who was missing, one name, that of Rydell, came up several times.

197

Though a loner and not popular, he had certain haunts and his absence from these was noted. The more he considered the idea, the more Malone was convinced that Rydell had been the killer. He was also sure that Wilson had been killed for the gun he wore rather than his money. If he was right, Grigg was in the area and Rydell knew where to find him. Whatever way he looked at it, he had to find Rydell.

'You're letting this Grigg business get to you,' Sheriff Harper told him when he visited him. 'Keep an open mind. Look at all the possibilities before you decide which track your investigation will take.'

'Maybe,' the new deputy admitted, 'but I know that Rydell was a crook when he was an army packer. I didn't recognize him in town, but I know the name. The bartender at the Gilded Lily also saw him talking to a gunslinger I saw in town the other day. I think he heard of the price that Grigg offered for the hides of Wilson and myself and the return of his gun.'

'But why would he suddenly kill Wilson?'

'Because he knows where Grigg is or will be, and reckons he's close enough to collect the reward that was offered.'

'So you really think Grigg would come all this way to get you?'

'He might, but I also know that this town's bank could be a temptation while he is around here. Seeing as he's in the vicinity, Grigg would be tempted to rob the bank. If he's getting another gang around him he'll need money to keep them with him. He wouldn't need a gang just to shoot me.'

'As far as I know,' Harper said, 'Wilson was an honest gambler, but all gamblers make enemies among losers. There are plenty of fools hanging around saloons ready to blame gamblers for cheating them when really they were too stupid to play the game properly. The killer could be a local man and it could be Rydell, but don't complicate things by bringing in Jonas

Grigg unless you know that he really was involved.'

'Maybe you're right, Sheriff. I'll concentrate on Rydell and see what he has to say for himself if I can catch up with him. I'll wire a few of the neighbouring lawmen and try to find out if they have seen him.'

'That's a good idea. You'll find a list of names and towns to contact in the top left-hand drawer of my desk at the office.'

'Well, I'd better get back to business, Sheriff. I'll keep you informed of what I find.'

After leaving Harper, Malone went straight to the livery stable where he found Hemings cleaning out the stalls.

'How's our new lawman going?' the livery-man greeted cheerfully.

'Still feeling my way, Mike. You might be able to help me. You see most of the horses that are around this town. Do you know what Rydell's horse was like?'

'Sure do. I sold it to him. It was an

ageing chestnut gelding about fifteen hands with a white nearside hind foot and a white star on its forehead and a snip on the nose. It had a Running M brand. Anything else you'd like to know?'

'Was it a good horse, the sort you'd take on a long ride?'

'Not really. It had a bit of tendon trouble and I sold it cheap. Rydell only wanted something for easy riding around town. A cowboy down on his luck gave it to me in payment for a feed bill. I had it here for months before Rydell bought it.'

'Do you know if Rydell kept it shod?'

'He should have, because that horse's hoofs were inclined to split, but I suspect he didn't always have the money. He picked up a bit of work recently though. He hired a wagon and a two-horse team from me. He was taking supplies out to a ranch.'

'Whose ranch?'

'He didn't say and I didn't ask, but he was out and back the same day.

Had a load of horse feed as well as the usual bacon and beans and flour and coffee.'

'Most ranches have their own wagons and do their own hauling. I wonder if he could have been stocking a camp somewhere for someone who normally doesn't need to have supplies on hand, someone like Jonas Grigg and his gang.'

Hemings thought for a while. 'It could be,' he admitted. 'An outlaw gang like Grigg's would use grain-fed horses and would have to keep them close at hand. They couldn't be turned out to graze like ranch horses.'

'If that's the case, our friend Rydell could have been in cahoots with Grigg. Chances are he helped set up a camp for them to operate from until they do their next raid. I know I sound obsessed but I think that Grigg is around here somewhere and he's planning some-thing.'

'If you're right they are within ten or fifteen miles of here. I know that because of the time Rydell was away with the wagon.'

'I think that abandoned line cabin that Pete Manson told us about is worth a look.'

15

'Just the man I wanted to see,' Hemings said when Malone came around to the stables the following morning. 'I had a visitor last night. Found him standing outside the stables when I came to open up.'

'Found who?' Malone was in a hurry and had no time for games.

'Rydell's horse turned up. This place is the nearest thing it had to a permanent home and I found it standing outside.'

'Was it saddled?'

'No, but it has been ridden recently. Its winter coat is matted up with sweat where a saddle would have been. Looks like it strayed from somewhere.'

Malone could not hide his disappointment. 'I was hoping to find Rydell, but it looks like he's got himself another horse. He won't hang around Rocky Creek now.'

'He surely won't,' Hemings agreed.

'Sorry I can't stay, Mike. I thought I'd just check on my animals and then send off some telegraph messages about Rydell. One of the other sheriffs might pick him up. Harper seems to think that's our best chance of getting him.'

'You don't sound so convinced.'

'I still think that old line cabin is worth a look. If nothing unforeseen happens in town I'm going out there today to have a look at it. Maybe it's in ruins and no use to anyone but I need to be sure.'

'You still think that gunman we chased might be holed up out there, don't you? You really hated letting him get away.'

'I did,' Malone admitted, and I have the feeling that we might be on to something more than just a spur-of-the-moment shooting.' As an afterthought he added, 'I might as well have a look at that horse's feet while I'm here, too, just so I can recognize his tracks if I come across them.'

'He's in the corral at the back. Help yourself.'

The chestnut horse was lean and even the winter coat did not conceal the ribs that were showing. It had seen more dinnertimes than dinners. The front hoofs were overly long and because of lack of trimming they were starting to chip. The gaps in the hoof wall showed clearly on the prints left in the dirt of the corral. He would be easy to track.

Malone arranged for the telegraph messages to be sent, then checked that all was well in the town before hurrying back to the stables for his horse. He stuffed a few biscuits in one saddle-bag and a supply of jerky and a box of rifle ammunition in the other to balance it. As an afterthought he emptied a part box of rifle shells into the big patch pocket on his blanket-lined, canvas coat. He was hanging the leather case for his field-glasses from the saddle horn when Hemings came along.

'You look like you're going somewhere, Jeff.'

'You're right there. I'm going out to have a look at that old line cabin and see if anyone has used it lately.'

'It might be hard to find if it is only a ruin,' Hemings suggested.

'I know but I need to satisfy myself that nobody is hiding out there.'

'What if you walk into trouble out there? You really need someone with you.'

Malone shook his head. 'I'm only going out for a look around. I don't intend starting a war. If things don't look right, I'll come back and get a posse.'

Hemings looked doubtful. 'That's if you're able to get back. If you strike Grigg and a couple of his friends, they might prefer to keep you out there one way or another.'

'You have a point, but I can't justify taking men away from their regular work just on suspicion. I'll make a deal with you: if I'm not back here by the time you lock up tonight, raise a posse and come looking for me tomorrow. You know the general direction of where I'm headed.'

'I still think you're crazy, but good luck.'

Malone led his horse out of the stable and swung into the saddle. 'See you tonight, Mike.'

He cantered out of the town and set a course for Duncan's Creek. The bay horse was fresh and eager to travel. Steam came from its nostrils as it snorted in the chill air. A couple of miles out of town, the trail was less hoof marked and the scout started looking about for tracks. To his surprise he quickly found the distinctive prints left by Rydell's horse. They were coming straight down the road from the opposite direction. Normally a loose horse wanders from one patch of grazing to another, but being winter not much feed was available and the chestnut had headed straight for town, a place it associated with being fed.

The day was bitterly cold and, after the recent blizzard, large patches of snow still remained, showing up a startling white against the grey sage and red earth. Malone pulled his collar higher around his ears as he studied the ground. Rydell's horse had stayed on the road.

Two hours later, he splashed through the freezing water of Duncan's Creek where it crossed the road. He had expected to see the horse tracks continue, but suddenly they were gone. He turned Major and cast about studying the ground with the intensity of a hunting dog. Much to his relief, he found the tracks again running parallel to the creek. The animal had followed the creek out of the tangled hills along its winding course.

Then he saw the tracks of a wagon and remembered what Hemings had said about Rydell hiring one. This immediately confirmed his hunch that Wilson's killer was not acting on his own. There were tracks of other horses along the wagon route too, clear, sharp-edged tracks indicating that the animals had all been shod recently. Somebody was getting ready for long, hard riding and was leaving nothing to chance. Malone was not sure how many riders there were as the tracks were intermingled but he estimated that there were at least four.

The creek meandered through what in summertime would be grassy flats flanked by high, sharp-edged ridges to which stunted pines and cedars clung precariously. It was ideal country for an ambush and anyone approaching along the creek was exposed to several vantage points where riflemen could lay in wait. It was asking for trouble to follow the creek.

He halted in a patch of leafless cottonwoods, dismounted and took out his field-glasses. The area had been old cattle country and he knew that, of all animals, cattle always followed the easiest trail through rough country. The trail might twist and turn but cows always followed the easiest grades. He had to get out of the bottom land around the creek. Because it had been necessary to build a line cabin, he knew that cattle had once grazed the area, so some of their old paths to higher country probably still existed. Once a regular track was made, wild animals also used it as the easiest way to water and grazing.

It took a while but eventually he caught sight of a narrow path following a zig-zag course up a sharp ridge to the left. From there he hoped to keep the creek in sight. He found the end of the trail behind a clump of hackberry bushes. It bore the prints of the deer that still used it but no signs of any horses. The grade was not steep although in places there were sheer drops to the valley below if a horse should slip. Malone remounted and as sure-footed as a cat, Major calmly picked his way through these dangerous sections. The rider left the animal's head alone knowing that it would

211

choose the safest path.

The ground eventually levelled out and Malone found himself looking at a sheltered plateau. He could see the other trail below the creek and the deep gouges in the soil showing where a wagon had struggled up a steep pinch to the higher level. The flat area was about half a mile long and the same distance wide and was lightly timbered. It had probably been open ground in the ranching days but now the forest was starting to reclaim it. Young pine trees and bushes were scattered all around the flat. He dismounted and scanned the area with the field-glasses. Eventually he saw the roof of the line cabin showing through the trees at the far end of the level ground. A tarpaulin had been used to repair it and the canvas showed plainly against the weathered shingles, a sure sign that someone was using it. For several minutes he studied the scene but could see no sign of life. He would have to move closer.

Malone remounted and cautiously rode down the steep hillside, keeping to the pines as much as he could. Upon reaching level ground, he found a patch of boulders with a few bushes around them and concealed his horse there. He munched a few biscuits from his saddle-bag as he viewed the scene from his new vantage point.

Across the flat, movement caught his eye. A man in a red and black checkered coat was sitting smoking on a rock. He had a rifle beside him and was watching down the trail beside the creek. Had his natural caution not warned him that the trail was a potential ambush site, he would have ridden straight into the sentry's gun.

Leaving Major hitched to a small tree, he took his carbine and field glasses and crept closer to the line shack while making sure that he kept out of the sentry's sight. The flat area where the cabin was situated had once been cleared but with the cattle gone, pine seedlings, other trees and bushes had encroached on it providing ample cover for a stealthy approach. Taking advantage of every bit of natural cover, the scout moved carefully to where he finally had an unobstructed view of the building.

He could see that the shack had been repaired just enough to provide some shelter from the weather. A couple of empty grain sacks had been nailed across the windows to keep out the worst of the wind. They prevented him from seeing into the building but also stopped those inside from seeing out, thereby reducing his chance of being seen. The corral attached to the back of the structure had been roughly repaired and there were several horses in it. He could not see them all, but immediately recognized the tall iron grey he had seen with the gunman in Rocky Creek.

A man came to the cabin's open door and gazed around as he cut a piece of chewing tobacco from a plug he was holding.

Malone found himself looking straight at Jonas Grigg.

Elation surged through him. He had been right. Grigg was connected to the strange events in Rocky Creek. Malone had located the enemy and his next task was to calculate their strength. He knew there were at least three men but wanted to count the horses or the saddles if he could see them. Lowering his field-glasses and clutching his carbine, he slipped into a small ditch and, bent double, was working his way to where he could see into the corral. Then things went wrong.

16

He heard yelling and it was coming from behind him where he had left his horse. Someone had found it.

'Look out!' a voice called. 'We got ourselves a visitor.'

Malone looked in the direction of the voice and saw two men leading his horse towards the cabin. Grigg appeared at the cabin door with two others. All were carrying carbines.

Conlon and Haskins had been out on foot looking for a deer to shoot when Malone arrived. Both sides had been moving stealthily and neither had suspected the presence of the other until the two outlaws found the horse.

'How many are there, Abe?' Grigg bellowed.

'Just one,' the other replied. 'We found his horse. He's here somewhere.'

'Stay where you are, Jud, and look

sharp,' the outlaw boss called again. 'Bring the horse here, Abe.'

Malone was trapped. Haskins and Williams, the sentry, had cut off his escape route. Elkins and Reece had moved to positions where they could cover parts of the flat. Each slipped into the brush so they would not afford easy targets.

Conlon brought the horse to Grigg and the outlaw searched the saddle-bags in an attempt to discover the identity of the man who had penetrated their hideout. When he saw the name J. Malone written inside the lid of the field-glasses case, he burst out laughing. His luck was in. The scout had obligingly fallen into his clutches. After placing the horse in the corral, he shouted, 'Nice of you to drop in, Malone. Saved me coming to look for you. This surely must be my lucky day. You might as well surrender, you won't get out of here alive.'

Malone stayed quiet unwilling to disclose his position until it became necessary. His enemies all had carbines and he was in range of them all. They had scattered, too, around the perimeter of the flat so that he was unlikely to get out of the area unobserved. The scout had plenty of cover but the outlaws had the numbers to flush him out.

Reece was the first one to start shooting. He fired two quick shots at what he imagined was a man. The bullets came nowhere near Malone.

'Did you get him?' Haskins called.

'Don't know,' Reece called back. He was reluctant to admit that he had panicked and fired wildly.

'Keep under cover, you jackasses,' Grigg yelled. He had set an example by crouching behind a sizeable stump, but the younger members of the gang had never been involved in such a situation. Confident in their numbers neither Reece nor Haskins had sought cover.

'I think I see him,' Haskins called and raised his rifle.

A shot cracked from the undergrowth

and the outlaw's leg buckled under him. Malone had decided it was time to reduce the odds and maybe shoot a hole in the cordon that was around him.

Elkins saw the powdersmoke and raked the area with shots from his repeater. But Malone had foreseen such action and was safely in a small dip in the ground. The bullets sang viciously, cutting off bushes above him but all were too high.

Haskins had recovered from the shock and was groaning in pain. Leaving his rifle where he had dropped it he began crawling back towards the cabin. 'Help me,' he called to his comrades. 'I'm bleedin' real bad.'

Grigg cursed quietly with rage. The last thing he wanted was to lose men before he hit the bank at Rocky Creek. His careful planning was coming apart. In his mind he had already written Haskins out of the plan. A wounded man was an encumbrance he did not need.

Dazed with pain and seeing the blood gushing from a severed artery in his broken thigh, the wounded man called for help again, but none of his comrades came. All were reluctant to expose themselves to the hidden scout in case they became his next victims.

Malone could see the wounded man from where he lay hidden and was quite prepared to kill anyone who came to his aid, but the outlaws knew that and left Haskins moaning on the ground. Gradually the moans faded as the outlaw lapsed into unconsciousness. Death would soon follow.

Abe Conlon peered cautiously over a log in time to see a slight movement of bushes about a hundred yards from where he had positioned himself on a piece of rising ground. He threw his carbine across the log but Malone saw him and beat him to the shot. The scout's bullet missed, but it tore a long sliver of wood from the log inches from Conlon's face. Involuntarily the tall gunman flinched and his return shot went wide.

Reece and Elkins both saw the gunsmoke, aimed below it and fired.

Malone was levering a fresh cartridge into the breech when a bullet tore the rifle from his hands. At first the scout thought he had been hit in the hand but a glance showed all his fingers intact although they were numbed by the impact. Much to his dismay he saw that a bullet had dented the brass receiver of the carbine bending it inwards. The breech was jammed in a partially opened condition and he could not close it. His Winchester was now useless. To make matters worse, a few more shots came in and landed dangerously close to him. He rolled away to the shelter of a small erosion gully leaving the useless rifle behind.

'I reckon we got him,' Elkins called.

'Be careful, Ike,' Grigg shouted back. He knew that the little gunman was inclined to be trigger happy and took risks that more prudent men would deem unacceptable. So far he had been lucky.

'You're getting scared in your old age, Jonas,' Elkins called, casually. 'He won't cause you any trouble now.'

'Stay down,' Grigg ordered, but Elkins felt that he needed no advice when it came to gunfighting. Standing erect with his Winchester thrust out before him, the little outlaw began advancing through the low brush. He walked into the sights of Malone's sixgun.

The scout peered from under a bush holding his big Colt in both hands. Thirty yards was a long shot for a revolver but Malone had a steady rest and a clear view of his target. He would have liked the outlaw to come closer but could not afford to be seen. Gently he squeezed the trigger. The gun kicked in his hand and Elkins was punched backwards, the hat flying from his head as he fell. The shot had been a bit high striking the outlaw near the chin, skidding along his jawbone and cutting a piece from the lobe of one ear. The shock of the wound temporarily put Elkins out of the fight.

Grigg could not believe his bad luck. He needed every man he had and now it seemed that two of them were out of action. He could not afford to be hampered by wounded men.

'That was a sixgun,' Conlon called. 'Are you out of rifle ammunition, Malone?'

The scout dared not give away his position by replying. He had hoped that none of the outlaws would note his change of firearm but Conlon was a professional gunfighter and missed nothing with regard to weapons.

Elkins sat up, felt his bloodstained face and winced as he touched his wounded ear. He untied his bandanna and dabbed at his wounds.

Grigg saw his associate struggling to get to his feet and was greatly relieved. 'Are you gonna live, Ike?' he called.

'I'll live longer than the sonofabitch

who did this,' the little outlaw replied, vehemently.

'You've got no chance, Malone,' Conlon called. 'We can keep out of range and kill you with rifles. If you give up, I'll talk Jonas into sparing your life.'

Seeing this as the best way out of a bad situation, the outlaw leader announced, 'That's right, Malone. We done deals before. You know I keep my word.'

No reply came from the brush.

'This is your last chance, Malone.' Grigg could not keep the frustration out of his voice.

Still silence.

'We could go in there and get him,' Reece suggested. 'There's five of us.'

Grigg ignored him. He could not afford to lose another man and had no intention of letting Malone know this. He had another idea. 'Someone climb a tree and see if you can see over that second-growth brush. He can't reach you with a six-shooter.'

Being the youngest and most agile,

Reece jumped into the branches of a nearby pine. Awkwardly juggling his carbine, he climbed higher being careful to keep most of the trunk between him and the man he sought. Suddenly he shouted, 'I can see him!'

Warned by the shout, Malone rolled sideways as a slug tore up the dirt where he had been lying. The move shifted the tops of some bushes and Grigg triggered a couple of shots in the general direction.

Reece fired again but his perch was not the steadiest. Again the shot missed but only by a narrow margin.

Malone sighted a narrow erosion gully a few yards away. It offered better protection than where he was and he made a flying dive for it. Another shot kicked dirt from the bank of the ditch as he rolled against it. Now he had another problem. His enemies could not see him, but he could not see them. An outlaw with the necessary degree of stealth could work quite close to him before being discovered. He looked at the sky and was thankful for the short winter day. When night fell he had a better chance of slipping out of the encirclement.

Conlon crept around to where Grigg was positioned. Bending low, he whispered, 'We got us some bad trouble here, Jonas. It's gonna cost us men if we have to flush him out. From what I've seen Malone doesn't miss too often. He damn near shot Ike's head off. What if we leave Reece and Williams here and we go to rob the Rocky Creek bank?'

Grigg shook his head. 'Reece don't have the brains of a gopher. He's a cow-thief and needs someone to tell him what to do. Williams knows the game, but I've noticed he's getting a bit nervy of late. He was good, but I think Malone would still have a good chance of getting the two of them. We can't risk leaving that coyote alive. It's gonna be a cold night. Maybe a few hours out in the frost might force that bastard to do something rash.'

'You're forgetting one thing, Jonas.

We can only keep Malone out in the cold by being out there ourselves.'

'I know, but we can get blankets from the cabin. We won't freeze but he just might.'

Malone had been inching his way through the brush being very careful not to be seen by Reece who was still in the tree and firing the odd shot in the hope of finding a target. He was close enough to hear the muted voices of Conlon and Grigg although he could not discern what they were saying. The gaps in the cordon had widened while the two older bandits were conferring and he carefully sought a means of slipping away. The light was almost gone when he found himself near the body of Haskins. Then he remembered something else: the outlaw had been carrying a carbine. Where was it? Eventually he sighted the weapon lying in a patch of long, frost-scorched grass. It was actually closer to him than it was to its late owner. A five-yard dash would bring him to the weapon. If he continued running he could break through the cordon provided a lucky shot in the bad light did not bring him down. Another thought also occurred to him. If he made the tree-line safely, he could command the trail which was the only easy way to get horses out of the area. He knew that Hemings would be there in the morning and the outlaws could be trapped. But first he had to get the Winchester and then had to dodge bullets until he reached the trees.

'There he is!' Reece shouted from his tree. The angle was an awkward one for him and it took a while to get the first shot away. It missed and the watchers saw Malone snatch up the rifle and make a zig-zag run for the darkness of the trees.

The outlaws fired, the red muzzle flashes of their rifles slashing through the gathering darkness. But luck was on the scout's side. He heard something zip past his head and a bullet plucked at his sleeve but he managed to throw himself behind the trunk of a big pine tree. As he did so another bullet struck the trunk but could not penetrate the solid wood. Levering a round into the breech, he snapped a shot back at the closest muzzle flash. 'Now you mangy coyotes,' he called in triumph, 'come and get me.'

17

Mike Hemings was a worried man. He knew that Malone should have been back by nightfall and he lingered at the stables watching every rider who rode into town. Although he had not discounted the possibility, he had never really expected that Malone would strike trouble on what was basically a trip of exploration.

He went home and had his dinner but could not relax.

'Mike,' his wife said, 'you're pacing around like a caged bear. Jeff will be all right.'

'I'm not sure he is, honey. If all went well he'd be back by now. I'm going up to see Tom Crane. I think I should get a few men together and ride out Duncan's Creek way.'

Crane was eager to go and would have set out there and then but

Hemings told him that little could be done in the dark. 'Just bring a rifle and a six-shooter and be at the stables at four o'clock. I'll loan you a horse and saddle.'

'I'll be there. Are you getting anyone else?'

'Yes. I hope to get Jack Hallam and Bill Wiess. They're old buffalo hunters and are handy with guns.'

'So you think there will be shooting?'

'I don't know what to think, Tom, but it pays to be prepared. Something's wrong, I know that much. I'll see you at four o'clock.'

'What's happening?' Nancy asked her husband, after Hemings had left.

'Mike thinks Jeff could be in trouble. We're going out looking for him in the morning.'

Julie came hurrying from the kitchen. She had overheard the conversation. Distress showed plainly on her face. 'Has something happened to Jeff?'

'We're not sure,' her brother told her gently. 'He's overdue back here in town.

In the morning a couple of us are going out to look for him.'

'I'll come with you.'

Crane put his arm around her. 'Not this time, Sis.'

'You think something bad has happened,' she accused. 'That's why you don't want me to come.'

'We don't know what's happened,' Nancy said, 'but we know that Jeff is a pretty resourceful character. He'll turn up. Just wait.'

'I wish I could be sure of that.'

★　★　★

The outlaws had retreated to the cabin. There was little to be gained by swapping shots outside. Reece was strongly in favour of a direct attack, but the more experienced ones knew that such tactics would be costly and success was by no means certain.

'What do you reckon we should do?' Grigg asked Conlon.

'That depends on what Malone does.

232

He has no horse and it's a long way to town. If he sets out to walk we might be able to ride him down along the road in a couple of hours' time. Meanwhile, we need at least two men guarding the corral to stop him getting his hands on a horse. Rather than wait around in the frost, I think he'll set out walking even if it's only to keep warm. Later we might be able to run him down on the road or at least get ahead of him and rob the bank before he gets to town. You don't have to kill him straight away, Jonas. I think the bank is more important at this stage.'

'You could be right, Abe, but we can't hit the bank until it opens and Malone, even walking, could get there ahead of us. Chances are, he's on his way now.'

'Maybe not, he's the sort of cuss who would lie up somewhere with a rifle and try to pick off a couple of us . . . and he's got another rifle now.'

'But we don't know how much ammunition he has. He might only have what's in the magazine.'

'Seems to me,' Williams told them, 'that not knowing what Malone is likely to do is the cause of all our trouble. I'm for going out after him if he is still outside. It's no use sitting here like a bunch of scared old ladies.'

Angrily, Grigg turned on him. 'Go right ahead, big mouth, and if you get your fool head blown off we'll know that he's still about. Go on. Go outside if you're so damn smart.'

His bluff called, Williams screwed up his fraying courage. He jammed his hat firmly on his head, picked up his carbine and walked to the door of the shack. He paused a second to glare defiantly at his companions and, as he turned again, a rifle cracked and a .44 slug buried itself in the doorpost about two inches from his ear and a splinter of wood hit him in the face. In his rush to get back under cover Williams tripped and sprawled full-length on the cabin floor.

'Any more bright suggestions?' Grigg asked him.

'At least we know he's still there,' Conlon observed. 'The big question is why. He's had a chance to run and he's still staying around. Something's wrong around here. He knows something that we don't.'

'Maybe he just wants his horse back,' Reece suggested.

An angry glare from his leader was sufficient to let the young man know that his opinions bore little weight.

Being free to move about gave Malone time to select a good position. It was where the outlaws had placed their sentries. Partially protected by boulders, a man could cover the main trail out of the area and had a good view all the way to the cabin. Even if he had wanted to, it would have been too cold to sleep so he resolved to annoy his enemies as much as possible. Three hundred yards was the accurate limit for a Winchester, but even in poor light he could still hit the cabin. The outlaws were not showing any lights but they had a fire going and its faint glow showed through the sacking tacked over the open windows. The first shot he fired thumped solidly into the logs, but the second found the sacking and buried itself in an inner wall inches from where Elkins was trying to sleep. A faint bar of light showed above the door and knowing that it would be of lighter timber, he had a couple more shots and must have hit the door at least once. All lights vanished as the outlaws were forced to extinguish their fire. Two bullets through the openings added little to the peace of mind of those sheltering inside. If Malone had to spend a sleepless night in the cold and frost, he saw no reason why his enemies should rest in comparative comfort. At irregular intervals through the night, he fired at the cabin. A couple of shots penetrated the door and the window and did little for the nerves of those inside.

By 5 a.m. Conlon had had enough.

Gritty-eyed and short tempered, he cursed and went to the back window where he began ripping away the sacking from the frame.

'You're lettin' in the cold,' Reece complained.

'That's bad luck,' Conlon growled. 'But I'm going out through the horse corral. He won't see me leave the cabin because he'll be watching the door. I'm going to work around to the hills at the bottom end of the flat to where we found his horse. He found a way to get there that took him around our guard. I've figured that he must be shooting from somewhere near where we posted a look-out. If I can backtrack from where he left his horse I might be able to get a shot at him from the hill above.'

'How are you gonna see him in the dark?' Williams asked.

'It will take me about an hour to work my way around there and it will be light by then.'

'That's a real good idea,' Grigg said, as he climbed out of his blankets. 'What do you want us to do?'

'When I get out of the window, show a bit of light inside the cabin. If he's watching that, there's a good chance I can get out the other side of the corral without him seeing me. If we can draw his fire I'll have a good idea of where he is.'

Conlon slipped out the window into the corral and crawled across it. He was wriggling out under the bottom rail when someone in the cabin showed a glimmer of light. He heard the shot and saw the muzzle flash. It told him that Malone was right where he hoped he would be.

★　★　★

Hemings led the group away a few minutes after the appointed time. He had saddled his best horses for Crane and himself and Hallam and Wiess were both mounted on serviceable animals. He was pleased that they had been able to join him as both were seasoned frontiersmen who had tangled both with Indians and outlaws in their careers. Crane was an unknown quantity but Malone had spoken highly of his performance at the stage station. His powerful .50/.70 rifle was only a single shot but it could outrange the Winchester and Henry carbines the others carried.

They timed their ride to perfection and, as the first red streaks of dawn appeared on the eastern horizon, they were splashing their mounts through the icy waters of Duncan's Creek.

From somewhere ahead they heard the distinctive crack of a Winchester. They paused and listened, but there were no other shots.

'I wonder who's shooting at what,' Tom Crane muttered.

'He might have hit whatever it was,' Wiess growled. 'Don't sound like anyone's shootin' back.'

'Malone has a Winchester,' Crane said hopefully.

'So does just about every man and

his dog in these parts,' Hallam reminded him. 'And them that ain't have got Henrys that shoot the same bullets.'

Hemings quickly picked up the trail. 'Look here, wagon wheels and horses have been up here along the creek. It's getting lighter now so we can follow them up. Keep your eyes peeled. We don't know who's ahead and this would be an easy place to spring an ambush.'

They moved ahead warily and were almost at the steep pinch just before the plateau when Hemings raised his right hand. 'I just saw a bit of movement in the trees on top of that rise ahead.'

A Winchester spoke from somewhere nearer and, as they watched, a man showed briefly among the rocks.

'I think that's Malone,' Hemings said.

'If it is, he's in trouble,' Hallam said, and pointed to a hill overlooking the man in the rocks. A rifleman was creeping along the crest, his eyes fixed on the scout below.

18

'Looks like he's fixin' to bushwhack the *hombre* below,' Wiess said.

'Not if I can help it,' Crane declared. He slid from his saddle and slipped a big brass cartridge into his rifle. Raising the peep-sight hinged on the small of the stock, he asked, 'What range do you reckon?'

'A good four hunnert yards,' Wiess said.

'I reckon it's about that, too,' Hemings told him. 'It's too far for a Winchester.'

'This is no Winchester,' Crane reminded them, as he made the necessary adjustments to the rear-sight. Then he seated himself on the ground with his knees up and his elbows resting on the inside of his knees.

'He's getting ready to shoot,' Hallam said.

Crane eased back the hammer, sighted quickly and squeezed the trigger. The Remington roared and a cloud of smoke leapt from its barrel. About a second later, the watchers saw the rifle fly from the target's hands as the big bullet knocked him down.

'Good shootin'.' Hallam clapped Crane on the back. 'I don't know if he's dead but he sure as hell won't be shootin' anyone.'

Malone heard the shot and turned to see the horsemen galloping toward him. He recognized Hemings in the lead and waved his hat. A short while later, they halted their mounts beside him.

'I'm sure glad to see you fellas,' he greeted. 'What was that shot?'

'Someone on that hill over there was getting ready to take a shot at you, but Tom got him first. It was a lovely shot and just in time,' Hemings explained. 'What's happening here?'

'Grigg and a couple of others are in that cabin over there. I've been annoying them waiting for you to turn up. I killed one of his men last night and think I wounded another.'

'You've been busy,' Hemings said. 'But they might not all be in the cabin now. We know that at least one of them got out.'

'There's a window on the other side that opens on to a corral. He must have got out through there,' Malone explained.

*   *   *

Inside the cabin, the outlaws were puzzled.

'It sounded like one of them big army rifles to me,' Elkins mumbled through the improvised bandages that swathed his face. 'Abe had a Winchester. I think Malone's got help.'

'So do I,' Grigg admitted. 'That's why that polecat hung around. He knew that help was coming. I think we need to get out of here while we still can.'

'You reckon they might surround the

cabin?' Williams asked, anxiously. Life on the wrong side of the law had suddenly lost its appeal. The outlaw's courage seemed to be draining from him.

'They will if they get the time and have the numbers,' Grigg told him. 'Go out the window and start saddling horses.'

'But if anyone's out there, they'll shoot me.'

'Suit yourself, you yeller dog,' Grigg turned to Elkins. 'Come with me, Ike, and we'll do the saddlin'.' To Reece and Williams he said, 'Keep a sharp look-out here and pick off anyone you see.'

The two older outlaws went out the window quickly and caught their horses. Their luck was holding and they were still sheltered by the cabin. As he cinched on the saddle, Grigg whispered to Elkins, 'When we're ready we're leaving here. Those two jackasses in the cabin will keep Malone busy while we sneak away.'

'You mean we ain't gonna tell 'em

we're goin', Jonas?'

'You're dead right, Ike. They can be useful for the first time in their lives right where they are. The longer the law thinks we're in that cabin, the better our chances are.'

When the horses were saddled, both men led them quietly to the corral rails that formed the gate. Being careful to make as little noise as possible they replaced the rails as they passed through. Loose horses would betray their plan so none of the others could be allowed to escape.

'Tell us when you want us to come out,' Reece called from the cabin.

Grigg did not reply, but looked at Elkins, put an index finger to his lips and led his mount away.

★   ★   ★

'I think we should cover the back of that cabin as quickly as we can,' Malone said. 'They might not be so easy to shoot if they get to their horses.'

245

Hallam and Wiess agreed and volunteered to gallop across the flat and cover the corral from the western side. Crane, on the eastern side, was given the task of putting the odd shot through the cabin door or window. Malone and Hemings set out on foot to cover the southern side. The cabin had no exits on the northern side and the country there was too steep for a horseman to escape in that direction.

'Let's go,' Hallam called to his friend, and set spurs to his big bay horse. They crossed the open trail and dashed into the brush on the plateau, their horses propping and wheeling around clumps of brush while the riders half expected to be met with a hail of lead from the cabin windows when they reached a point where they would be visible.

The hail of lead met them but from directly in front. Unknowingly, they had ridden straight at Grigg and Elkins. The outlaws, thinking they had been discovered, let loose a stream of lead from their repeaters as the riders came into view. Hallam was punched back over his horse's rump, landing in an untidy tangle of arms and legs. Wiess felt two shots hit his mount but dragged up its head and it staggered a few yards further before collapsing in a heap. Diving clear of the stricken animal, he rolled behind a stump. He had lost his rifle in the fall and drew his revolver as he sought a target.

'Stay here and shoot anyone you don't know,' Malone told Crane. He called to Hemings, 'The others have struck trouble. It's best we go in there on foot, but we'll need to be careful we don't shoot each other. There's four of us and an unknown number of them all in a fairly small area.'

'I can see a horse's back over the brush ahead and a bit to your left,' Crane called.

As Malone slipped into the brush he tried to keep Hemings in sight, but each man chose a different path and they were soon separated. A deadly game of hide-and-seek started.

19

'Jack, where are you?' Hemings called.

'I think Jack's hit,' Wiess called back from about fifty yards away somewhere to his left.

Malone kept silent and listened for the trampling of horses. He knew that the loose horse would probably join those that the outlaws were leading. The animal was scared and snorting as it forced its way through the brush.

Grigg cursed silently. The loose horse was a problem but there was no quiet way to be rid of it. The outlaws knew the approximate locations of Hemings and Wiess and quietly led their horses through the brush. They knew that once mounted, their heads would show above the greenery.

Elkins caught the loose horse's reins and hitched them to a young pine tree. If the animal became restless, it would shift about and move the tree top and this could be a useful diversion. He hung his carbine back on the saddle relying on one of his trusty Navy Colts which would be easier to use at close quarters.

Hemings found Hallam sprawled on his back with blood staining his upper body. The wounded man's eyelids fluttered, first in alarm, but then relief flooded across the pale features as he saw a friend. 'Mike,' he croaked.

Hemings laid a finger to his lips to indicate silence for he knew that the outlaws could not be far away, but the damage was done.

Elkins heard the voice and changed course. But he could not do it silently. A bush scraped along stirrup fender and the sound carried clearly. The hunters heard it too and both Wiess and Malone started to converge on the spot.

Grigg, who was following behind, mentally checked his options. They came down to two, fight or flight. He did not particularly fear a fight but enemies of unknown numbers and in unknown places made such action unlikely to succeed. Sudden flight with the element of surprise was hazardous but experience had shown that it was often a success because the enemy lost a few seconds. A fast horse could cover a lot of ground in that time, certainly enough to carry a man out of accurate pistol range. When Elkins looked around for directions, the outlaw leader pointed to his saddle indicating that they should mount and then pointed to the direction of the trail. They would make a mounted dash and try to flee back along Duncan's Creek.

Malone stretched out on the ground and peered beneath the low bushes. He found that he could see a fair distance. Something moved and he could just discern the fetlocks of a horse. A saddle creaked as someone mounted. Then the horse's feet turned toward him. Transferring his cocked Winchester to his left hand, he drew his Colt. There would be no time to lever cartridges into a rifle.

Crane was fast losing interest in the men in the cabin. They had not attempted to return his shots and he thought that they might have left the building by the back window. He glanced across the brush on the flat and to his surprise, saw the heads of two men suddenly appear as the outlaws mounted. He threw his rifle to his shoulder and fired. The shot went low but it struck Grigg's horse causing it to rear over backwards and spill its rider.

Malone heard the shot and the commotion that followed. He jumped to his feet just as Elkins, on a big, black horse, came smashing out of the brush. He fired the carbine one-handed, missed and snapped a revolver shot as the little outlaw leaned from his saddle and fired. The scout's shot told and Elkins swayed in his saddle losing control of his mount. In panic, the horse swerved throwing Elkins straight on to Malone and the pair crashed in a tangled heap. The little gunman slashed frantically with his gun barrel. It hit

Malone on the jaw as he tried to roll clear.

Despite his years, the little outlaw was as nimble as a cat and Malone saw the black muzzle of the Navy Colt trained straight at him. Even as he brought up his own gun he knew he would be too late. Then a look of surprise came to Elkins' face. He could not cock his gun. He was going for his left-hand revolver when Malone shot him through the chest. As the little outlaw fell, the scout was looking for Grigg. 'Got one,' he called for the benefit of his friends. Then he rapidly changed position.

Grigg's fallen horse was thrashing about, but the outlaw had crawled away from the scene. Like a wounded animal at bay, he sought a place where he could make a stand and do maximum damage to his enemies. He would never surrender.

Wiess had joined Hemings to assist the wounded Hallam. While one stood guard the other attended to the wound.

They found that the bullet wound was not a serious one, but Hallam had hit his head when knocked from his horse and was drifting in and out of consciousness. Both saw the need for a doctor, but decided that they should stay where they were to tip the odds in Malone's favour. Hemings actually moved a short distance away so that he could see over a larger area.

The loose, black horse, snorting nervously, trotted out of the brush and stood by the others in the corral. Grigg heard it going and knew that he had little chance of escaping on horseback, but he had escaped from similar situations before on foot. He had lost his rifle in the fall but still had a pair of sixguns and a reasonable supply of ammunition. He silently cursed Reece and Williams for a pair of cowards. Their presence could have tipped the fight in his favour but they appeared to be staying out of things. He saw nothing wrong in deserting them. He owed his longevity to his ability to decide when to support his friends and when to run.

Because of the hours spent in the same area the previous day, Malone had acquired a fair knowledge of that particular patch of brush. He knew the places where he had found the most shelter and decided to search them first. He was easing around a log when he saw movement through the leafless branches of a distant bush. He also knew that there was a shallow ditch behind the bush. The hairs on the back of his neck rose as though a hand was brushing them upwards. Peering around the end of the log, he knew that someone was in the ditch but it could have been one of his own men.

He decided to take a chance. Silently he rose until he was slightly crouched with the rifle at his shoulder.

'Throw out your guns, you're covered.'

Malone's call flushed the outlaw from cover. But he came out shooting. The scout got his shot away first and the rifle slug took a piece of Grigg's coat pocket. The near miss affected the outlaw's aim and his shot, at a fairly long range for a revolver, clipped a piece from a bush beside Malone's head. Firing rapidly, Grigg threw a few more hasty shots and charged forward to narrow the distance from his target. Malone's next shot hit him hard and threw him back against a small tree. One gun had fallen from his hand and he now struggled to raise the other, his face reflecting both the effort involved and his hate for the man who had shot him.

'Drop it, Grigg!' Malone called. He did not want to shoot again.

Another gun blasted from the brush and the wounded outlaw was smashed to the ground. Wiess arrived with his rifle ready for another shot. But none was needed.

'I got him! I killed Jonas Grigg.'

'You sure did,' Malone agreed.

20

Wiess was only too happy to ride to town to bring back medical help and a wagon for Hallam and the bodies. As the man who killed Jonas Grigg he would have acquired sufficient prestige to keep him in free drinks for quite a while.

Reece and Williams surrendered without a fight and under the watchful eye of Crane they helped drag the bodies out of the brush. All the fight they might have had was gone from them. Aware that hanging was a real prospect, they suddenly became co-operative. In the hope of more lenient treatment, they also volunteered to tell all they knew of the 'respectable' people who had been part of Grigg's organization.

Malone picked up the Navy Colt that had jammed at the crucial moment and cost Elkins his life. He showed it to Hemings.

'That's always a weakness with the percussion Colts,' he explained. 'Pieces of fired caps often fall into the workings and jam them. If that man had moved with the times I would be dead. The Navy Colt's a nice gun to shoot and is very accurate, but it's out-dated now.'

They walked across to where Crane stood guard over the prisoners.

'You did some pretty fancy shooting today, Tom,' Hemings said. 'I never knew you could shoot like that.'

'I used to shoot a lot of game for survey camps. All that practice came in handy today. According to the prisoners, we killed three badly wanted men and there could be big rewards involved. This little expedition could make us rich men if we split the money between us.'

'Suits me,' Malone said. He already had money coming from shooting Clem Ryan and Dakota. His share of the latest rewards would give him enough to start his own ranch.

'Thinking of settling down?' Crane asked.

Malone thought of Julie. 'Maybe,' he admitted.

THE END